D1569693

The Grimy and the Greedy

Meaghan Curley

Cosmic Teapot Publishing

Hanmer, ON

The Grimy and the Greedy

ISBN: 9781988762180

Copyright © 2020 by Meaghan Curley

Cover art by Emily Internicola

Published by Cosmic Teapot Publishing

Hanmer, ON, Canada

www.cosmicteapot.net

Ordering Information:

Quantity sales. Special discounts are available on quantity purchases by corporations, associations, and others. For details, contact the publisher at the email address above.

Acknowledgments are usually done in the back of the book. Not mine. I like to give thanks first to the people who made this novel a *much* better story: To Sal Piazza, Nikki Timmons, Chanel Hardy of *Hardy Publications,* and Carmen Loup, author of the fabulous *the Audacity* series for your invaluable insights and loving support. To Dylan Callens, who gave this book and her big sister, *Girl: Repurposed*, a home.

Thank you thank you thank you.

Also, shout-out to *the Topspin*, my long-gone childhood tavern, for inspiring this deranged ghost story.

Character List:

Fizzy—Eldest grandchild to Jeanette Sobriquet.
Government name is Odette Obiit.

Affidious Dixon—bartender/ owner of The Topspin. Also
known as Fiddy.

Zeno—Fizzy's roommate/ best friend. Also known as
Zenny and Jelly Buns. Government name is Džejla
Zenovenovic.

The Wraith—Bosnian-Serbian war criminal.

Darlene Sobriquet—Odette, Lonnie, and Tranquila's
mother. Daughter to Jeanette Sobriquet

Dr. Olivia Dixon—Affidious' mother.

Lonnie Obiit—Fizzy's brother.

Tranquila Obiit—Fizzy's sister.

Grandpa Claus—Fizzy and Zeno's downstairs neighbor.
Government name is Rocco Petito.

Tits—Regular customer at the Topspin/ Affidious' mail
carrier.

Travis—homeless homie

Joanna—Zeno's crush

Tonya Begic— Zeno's mother

Jeanette Sobriquet—Grandmother to Odette, Lonnie, and
Tranquila.

This book is for my best friend, Nikki. Merry Christmas!

TABLE OF CONTENTS

PART ONE: ANTI-GOING

Prologue:

Fizzy knew she fucked up when she woke up in a pothole. She felt the pebbles pinch the side of her face before she felt the scorching sunburn on her back. She was already ashamed and didn't know what for. Just like yesterday and the day before.

With a feeble push-up, she got to her knees and saw two homeless people fucking against a tree. It wasn't until she got to her feet and started walking up the hill that she remembered they were in the same spot yesterday. And the day before.

She slipped twice trying to get up the hill because she wasn't wearing shoes but managed to get back over the guardrail. Her socks were soaked with last night's rain but once they touched the sidewalk, they burned. She thought the cloth was going to melt into her flesh the heat was so intense. It wasn't until she started walking west that she noticed her back was screaming or that her hands were pulsating with errant blood. The longer she walked, the redder her clothes became. Yet, she wasn't alarmed. The sunburn, the blood, the scabs, the cuts. She was of a single mind: Hide. Find a way back home. And, if time permitted, kill Affidious before that fucker killed her first.

1.

Wednesday

It was early. The store called *Panzon's* had just opened mere minutes ago. There was still a sleepy haze hanging in the air as a handful of early morning shoppers meandered slowly underneath the shallow, fluorescent lights. In the back of the grocery store where the bakery department stood, you'd find a stringy twenty-seven-year-old white woman in an unflattering maroon-colored uniform with her shoulder-length sunset red-dyed hair pulled back into a bun and a face full of fire-ant red acne singing a made-up song under her breath as she shuffled her feet to stay awake.

It was the day before the end of an arduous sixty-hour workweek when she got the news. One of Fizzy's coworker's horses got spooked by a shadow and accidentally broke her coworker's leg and Fizzy foolheartedly jumped to cover the unmanned hours. By then, she was nearly delirious from exhaustion. But she was cheerful. For it was payday. Better yet, tomorrow would be her first day off, from both jobs, in nearly two weeks.

"I'm going to get a big ass check and I'm going to spend it on stupid shit," she sang tunelessly under her breath as she hurriedly sliced through a rack of fresh Italian bread. "I'm going to get a big ass check and I'm going to spend it on stupid—SHIT!"

Her gloved hand had slipped and got in the way of the blade.

She flung the knife onto the industrial countertop and held the throbbing digit inside her palm until she got to the automatic paper towel dispenser and wrapped a yard of stiff, brown paper around it. Blood blotted the black slab slated floor.

Her 'shit' was too loud. A little old lady passing by the cake shelves heard and laughed while a middle-aged man inspecting the Italian bread turned his head to glare.

Within seconds, the paper towel turned scab red. She unwrapped it to see how bad the cut was. *Shit*, she thought, more inconvenienced than upset. She was nettled at the thought of having to pay for stitches. With a frustrated growl, she ditched the bloody paper towel into a nearby trash can and washed it in an adjacent sink.

She had turned the sink off and reached for another paper towel when footsteps approached. She didn't have to turn around to know she was going to be irritated. A forty-something woman in the same berry red and khaki uniform stood by the oven.

"A customer heard you swear."

In another world, Fizzy would've opened her mouth, told Miss Karen to fuck off then flicked blood directly into the deli manager's mouth and cackled like a villain while Miss Karen freaked out. But this Fizzy held her bandaged finger up and explained, "Yeah. Sorry. I cut the sh—shellac out of my hand."

Miss Karen looked at her hand, then dropped her head, where more evidence of her injury laid, then looked back up at her, without a flicker of compassion in her face, and asked, "Is it bad?"

It feels fucking bad. "I don't know," Fizzy replied

Miss. Karen looked back down at the floor. "You gotta leave the department when you get cut. It's a biohazard."

Fuck you. "Sorry."

"I'll mop up the blood. Go to the first aid kit."

Fizzy squeezed her finger until she could feel her pulse beating through the coarse sheet and made her way out of the department, making sure to track footprints through the blood first. She held onto the finger carefully so she wouldn't accidentally spill throughout the rest of the store. On her way to the front of the store, she passed by the same old man who glared at her earlier and tried to force an uncomfortable shared gaze. The old man did not look up from his bag of organic pasta sauce, enthralled by the list of ingredients. A petty victory.

Working in a bakery isn't all cookies and sunshine. The most she got out of it was taste-testing and eating cake for breakfast (which she never got tired of). One of the few and infrequent perks of the job. That and the fellowship of frosting loving women who congregated to the department. And the small moments in between following standard practice and basic cake decorating designs where she got to be creative. The fluffy flowers. The creamy borders that call to mind seashells. Oh, and the colors. All the colors. From the gigantic frosting buckets that reminded her of sweet-smelling Play-Doh to the dye guns that gently sprayed rainbows onto vanilla canvases and leave your exposed flesh iridescent.

Fizzy meandered casually to the back office, wanting to take as much time as possible to feel bad for herself. It was a shit day. She had woken up at 3:15 in the fucking morning, left her warm fucking bed, just to go outside into the bitter bitch of Mid-March and drive with one hand firmly grasped onto her driver door's handle because the lock mechanism on her door didn't work in -5 degree weather, so it wouldn't close properly. She arrived at work in the blackened pre-dawn only to step out of her car and hear her phone fall onto the ground because she was too frazzled from sleep-deprivation and too cold to remember that she had the device on her lap. When she picked it up, she found a chunk of the right-hand corner of her phone screen was gone and so with it her good-natured mood.

A round-faced cashier, one of many part-time-working teens that filtered in and out of the company during the year, walked out of the breakroom and towards the punch-in-punch-out machine that hung off the back-office door. "Hey, girl." They said with a drawl as they typed in their number automatically. "You should check your phone. It's blowing up." They breezed away without further context. Fizzy didn't think anything of it, more offended by the cashier's total apathy towards her conspicuously bleeding injury. She washed her hand in the break room sink and wrapped a Dora the Explorer Band-Aid around the cut. Driblets escaped out of Dora's square-shaped hair but Fizzy put a latex glove over the hand and decided to ignore her bleeding and the pulsating.

She went to her work locker, which displayed her dreaded name, Odette Obiit, in scotch tape and black marker.

Upon opening, she discovered to her alarm that she had nine missed notifications:

--2 missed calls from Sis

--3 missed calls+1 missed voicemail from Mama Sobriquet

--3 missed texts from Bro-Bro of all which read: "Yo" "Fucko McGee" "Call mom"

Dread imploded within Fizzy like a bomb. What could be so urgent?

Before she could check her voicemail, a voice from behind alerted her that someone was calling them from the store's landline.

The breakroom and the manager's office were five steps apart but the entire way there, a litany of every possible bad thing went off in Fizzy's head: What if mom had been in a car accident? What if there had been a house fire? What if her apartment had caught fire? What if some unhinged man had attacked a loved one and left her beaten, bloodied, and moribund on the side of the road somewhere? What if something terrible had happened to Zeno or Tranquila or Lonnie?

By the time, she reached the landline, black and white images of her loved one's corpses—riddled with bullets, blood, and gaping wounds—filled her mind to the point where, while she held the receiving end of the phone to her ear, she choked back tears as she waited for the voice of Death to tell her all her favorite people on Earth were now His—

"Hey, sweetheart." Her mom's honeysuckle lilt sprang out of the other line in a tone she couldn't identify.

"Ma!" She was breathless with worry. "I was just about to call you. Is everything okay?"

"You didn't check your voicemail?"

"No. I just saw the calls. What's going on?"

There was a horrible pause. "Your grandma died."

For a moment Fizzy didn't comprehend. Part of her was convinced she misheard. "What?" Then she stalled, more disbelieved than shocked. It was like hearing the news that Satan just died. Up until that very moment, Fizzy was convinced that old, awful woman could never die. The same way evil and the dead can never truly die. "Are you messing with me?"

"No, sweetheart, I'm not messing with you. Jeanette's gone." Darlene said plainly for what else could be said. "She died this morning."

For a moment, there was nothing else said. Fizzy merely stood there, stupid from the surrealness of it all. She never thought this day would come. She, like many, assumed that her grandmother was one of the old witches that always got older but never would do something as impossible as dying. But then, it hit her all at once. Her grandmother, Jeanette Sobriquet, mother to her mother, grandmother of three, enemy to all, was dead. And when that realization came over her, Fizzy drew one long sweet breath in and her puffy lips curled into a wide, deranged smile. "I never thought this day would come." She squeaked out pink-faced, teary-eyed, and grinning. She held a hand over her heart, like she was trying to keep it from exploding, and exhaled out a breathy, almost delirious laugh. "I can't believe the bitch is dead."

"I couldn't believe it either...." Darla avowed but Fizzy talked over her, excitement bubbling out of her ears.

"I never thought I would get to outlive one of my enemies but…This is the greatest day of my life!" she exclaimed, unashamed.

"Are you even going to ask how she died?" Darla said.

"How did she die?!" Fizzy asked, flapping her unused hand from excitement. She gasped. "Oh my god. Was it murder or was it something stupid like she died in a car accident?" She let out another gasp. "Please tell me she got some horrible flesh-eating disease that takes away all your dignities."

"Nope. Believe it or not, the woman got struck by lightning."

"Damn. She would," she said, irritated. Though, quietly, she thought that the end was fitting. If anybody deserved to get smited by the Gods, it was Jeanette. Either way, it didn't matter. The bad times were over now. Jeanette was dead and their family was free from her. They could move on with their lives finally. "I'm just glad some of us got to outlive her."

"You're telling me," Darla said with a soft chuckle. "I was convinced that old biddy would bury us all."

"Nice. Good for you ma. I'm glad you're not wasting time being sad over that menstrual cramp of a woman."

"Oh…I'm a little sad."

Fizzy winced. "Really?"

"Well, yeah!" her mother replied as if it were obvious. "She was my mother after all. No matter how awful she was…" Her sentence died with a sigh. "It's still a loss. Even if it's more of a relief than anything."

Fizzy frowned into the phone. It hadn't occurred to her that her mother still cared for the old woman, especially after all she had put her through. "Oh…ma, I'm sorry ma…" She murmured. With nothing else to say, she asked, "How's Lonnie and TQ taking the news?"

She heard her mom sniffle, once, and Fizzy feared for a hot second that her mom was going to break down on her but then her voice came back, brighter than ever, as she said "Tranquila's right here if you want to talk to her." There was a quick exchange and soon, her sister's squeaky voice greeted her with a "Heyyyyy."

"Heyyyyyyyyy," Fizzy cried out. "What's up with you, TQ? Can you believe this?! Finally, after all these years, the wicked bitch of the west side is dead!"

"Wowwww. You are RUTHLESS!" Tranquila laughed. "You can't even pretend to be sad for once second."

Fizzy sucked her teeth. "Don't act like you didn't hate the woman either. Oh, wait. I forgot. She landed you a sweet job so now you're going to let eighteen years of child abuse go out the window."

"I mean…kinda," Tranquila admitted.

Fizzy scoffed.

"Dude I'm not like you," her sister said defensively. "I can't just cut people off like that. I'm like a dog. You could kick me and I still would love you."

Fizzy shook her head. "You're just like mom. Too forgiving." *But I guess there are worse ways to be,* she thought as she smiled into the phone. "Yo, since we're not doing a funeral for the old biddy, we should throw a death day celebration party! Like we always said we would!"

An awkward silence followed. One that made her immediately suspicious.

"That's the bad news," Darla's voice interjected from a nearby distance. "The funeral's Saturday."

"Ma, you're going to that?!"

"We all are. Including you."

"What? Nooooo!" Fizzy cried half-appalled and half-heartbroken. "I can't believe this bullshit! You're going to throw away money on a funeral for that woman?!"

"We're not throwing her anything…" Darlene's distant voice began but then there was more movement and her mother's voice returned, louder but as serious as ever. "She made the arrangements for the funeral before she died. Everything's all paid for. I didn't have to put a dime towards anything."

"Good!" Fizzy said.

"All we have to do is show up."

"We?!"

"C'mon Fizz!" Tranquila's voice shouted, clearer than before as she grabbed the phone. "If you don't go it's just going to be Lonnie, me, and mom."

"Then don't go!"

"I can't just *not* go to grandma's funeral! I lived with her for the last year of her life! Hell, I was there when she died!"

"So what?! I used to live with her too, that doesn't mean I'm going!"

"Please Fizzy please! Don't make me go to this thing alone."

"I would rather work!"

"C'mon… Don't do this. You know this is how ghosts are made," Tranquila pleaded. "You already know if grandma feels disrespected, she's going to come back and haunt the shit out of us."

It sounded irrational but Fizzy understood where the fear came from. The woman used to make that threat once a year on her birthday. But Fizzy wouldn't have it. "You don't believe in ghosts."

"No…" she admitted. "But I do think it's wrong to shit on a dead person's last requests."

"She disrespected us the entire time she was alive. Why should I let her bully me from beyond the grave?"

"I know you hated Grandma. But I didn't…"

"NO!"

She heard her mother's hand rush for the phone. Seconds later, Darla's voice, clear as water, heavy as stone, returned, "Odette—" She flinched at the sound of her government name. "Odette Elise Obiit. You are going to this funeral. End of discussion."

Fizzy balked. "The hell I am!" Frustrated tears leaked onto her uniform and she stood there, crying shamelessly into the phone, hating her mother, hating her whole family, hating her whole life. "I'm almost thirty years old! You can't make me go to this!"

"The hell I can't! I don't care how old you are—"

She croaked out, "I can't believe you're doing this to me."

"Odette, please." Her mother's voice sounded so pitiful. Like she was trying hard not to cry. "This isn't easy for me either…"

"Then why are you doing this at all?!" She furiously wiped away hot snot and tears, her voice getting pitchy the longer she raged. "It's not like anyone's going to come to this—"

"Oh, trust me. People are going to come to this."

"Then let them go! Why are you making me? Why are you letting her bully you like this from beyond the grave? She can't do anything to you anymore."

"I know that…"

"Do you though?" The question sprang out into the speaker like a jaded rock and landed on hot, terrible silence.

"I'm not doing this for her," Darla insisted unconvincingly.

Fizzy wanted to argue, to tell her, no, you're doing this because you're still that abused kid who has to let Jeanette get her way to avoid her rage. You're making us go because Jeanette needs to control everything and everyone, even if she's dead in the ground. But you don't have to let her do this. You're free now, she wanted to shout. She saw the words too, in front of her, like they were being held up on a banner. But she closed her eyes at them. Because you don't say cruel things to people you love. Even if they're true.

"You're going to this funeral," her mother said. "End of discussion."

Fizzy's face scrunched up tightly. Her cheeks were so hot, she thought the plastic on the old phone would melt.

2.

In a two-story off-white house with a dark green porch and a newly shingled roof, a flabby dark-skinned forty-six-year-old Black man with rust-colored hair and a bulbous nose riddled with blackheads laid on top of a blue yoga mat, grunting like an old man trying to get out of a chair. He was doing his best to keep up his sixty-nine-year-old mother, a lanky peach-faced woman with short gray hair who was following the instructions of the silly-string thin Asian woman talking on his smart TV with embarrassing ease. In the corner, a chunky tabby cat with an M shaped ear and one yellow eye watched them in the cool, dim living room with mild intrigue.

"Now we're going to go back down into the child's pose."

"Oh, thank fuck," he whispered to himself as he readily collapsed onto his knees, hands splayed above his bent head which he pressed gratefully against the freezing carpet. They were on day three of watching the same Yoga for Beginner's YouTube tutorial, per Olivia's physical therapist, and the only pose that got any easier was the child's pose.

"Out of the thousands upon thousands of words I know you know," Olivia said wryly with her aged dry wine of a voice. "You constantly choose the same four-letter vulgarities."

In his youth, her comment would've rubbed him the wrong way and, inevitably, would have procured a fight. But instead, her adult son turned his head toward her, and said, "Isn't brevity the soul of wit or some shit?"

Olivia shook her head, with a half-beleaguered sigh, then let out a raspy drawl of a giggle which endeared him more and more the longer they lived together. Soon, the pair dissolved into giggles. Something they never did in the past.

Once the laughter died, he tried to focus on his breathing, which was ragged after forty minutes of exercise, when he felt Miss Polly's wet nose rubbing against the tip of his ear, followed by the gentle graze of her sharp teeth. A breathless laugh burst out of Affidious.

He lifted his head only to be headbutted by the furry cyclops.

"You love me, Miss. Polly?" Affidious asked with mock scrutiny. "Or you just hungry?"

Miss Polly purred loudly as if to say, why not both?

Affidious let out one giant huff of relief as he struggled to his knees, announcing, "Okay. I'm done." He reached for his phone which lay on the coffee table nearby and turned to the kitchen. His body ached still from the day before, and it showed in his calves which trembled as he raised himself from the ground.

"Giving up already?" Olivia asked teasingly as she pushed herself up to emulate the instructor's warrior pose.

"I gotta feed the cat." He insisted as he limped towards the kitchen.

"Oh sure…blame the feline." Olivia grinned knowingly at the glowing screen and called out, "How does it feel to be more out of shape than your elderly mother?"

He turned on his heel, gave his sagging paunch a proud slap, and said, "Pretty damn good."

Olivia's laughter followed him and Miss Poly into the kitchen.

"I should've fed you when I woke up but I forgot," Affidious said apologetically in that low affectionate baby voice humans use with their pets. "I'm still new at this." Miss Polly trailed him, from a distance, for she was not certain whether there would be food at the end of this walk or a sharp kick but once the sound of a can being opened pricked her misshapen ears, she dashed to Affidious' ankles and began rubbing against his shins thankfully. Affidious shook the wet food into the cat's dish and placed it on the floor beside the refrigerator to give Miss Polly some privacy. Miss Polly beelined for the dish and Affidious went back into the living room to retrieve a half-drank coffee cup that he planned to reheat another two to three times before actually consuming the whole drink.

He was met with the violent sounds of his phone vibrating against his leg. When he took out his phone, a local number he didn't recognize popped up. He tapped the speaker on. "Hello?"

"Hello, I'm looking for Affidious Dixon?" An unfamiliar woman's voice asked.

"This is him."

"Um, hi. My name is Darlene Sobriquet. You don't know me but… you knew my mother?"

"Oh." He quickly took the call off the speaker and pressed the phone against his sweaty cheek. He looked over his shoulder to ensure his mother wasn't eavesdropping before he proceeded with awkward cheerfulness, "Hi."

"Hi," the woman returned, sounding like she was trying to conceal a sadness. "Um…I don't know how to tell you this but…uh, she passed away this morning."

"Oh…Wow." For a while, it was all he could manage to say. Then he realized his rudeness and added, "I'm..uh…I'm sorry."

"Thank you," Darlene said with a sigh, sounding as stressed as he imagined she was. "It's uh…it's… "

"Shocking," he blurted out without meaning to.

Thankfully, the woman let out a breathy laugh. Like she needed it. "I know…I always assumed she would outlive us all."

Like a cockroach or a crackhead, he thought but kept his lips tight as Darlene added, almost sheepishly, "But, um, yeah, I'm the executor of her estate and she has a letter for you. But the only address she put down was some bar…"

Affidious snickered. *Of course, that bitch would,* he thought, rolling his eyes.

"…I wanted to double-check before I sent it out…"

"No, the address she put down is correct," he told her with amusement but then added, so she wouldn't think he was just some degenerate drunk, "I own *The Topspin*."

"Oh? I thought that place was…"

"Nope, shockingly, it's still in business."

"Oh, um, well, g-great. I'll send it out today."

"I appreciate that." He said quickly. "And I am sorry for your loss. I can only imagine what you and your family are going through."

A small, hesitant pause came from the other end of the call. He waited for her to ask the obvious: How did you know my mom? How come I've never heard of you? How much do you know about that woman?

But she didn't ask anything. Instead, she said, "Thank you for your kind words. But, we both know, this wasn't much of a loss."

A stretch of silence lapsed between them. He was about to end the call when her voice popped up and said, "But it was nice talking to you."

"Same to you," he said. Then the call disconnected and he was left standing there, a laugh rising in his throat as his hand dropped down to his side. He turned his attention to Miss Polly who continued munching away on her canned food and whispered, tenderly, "I knew you were good luck kitty."

"Who was that?" Olivia asked as she veered towards the counter where her weekly pillbox sat.

"No one you'd know, Miss Nosy Parks," Affidious replied as he watched her fill a glass of water for herself. He waited until he watched her toss back the rainbow assortment of pills before he side-stepped to a hanging wall calendar and scribbled the time, 7:37 am, in the day's column.

Olivia narrowed her large, hooded brownie colored eyes at him then walked over and pinched his upper arm fat. "Smartass." Affidious feigned like she had stabbed him to which she pinched him again harder to which he let out an actual yelp of pain. But then they dissolved into fits of laughter and, for a moment, things were better than they ever were.

3.

Fizzy ran into the bathroom like she was being chased by a wraith as memories—ones she fought long and hard to dull—poured out of her like water from the broken dam. It wasn't until the stall door locked that she wept quietly into her fists. She did her best to keep her mouth tight, her sobs inaudible, for she would be damned if anybody caught her crying at work, let alone crying over Jeanette.

Then a hard knock came and rattled the door like a chain-linked fence caught in a storm. "Someone's in here," she said, in-between sniffles.

A second passed then came a second, harder, louder knock.

"Someone's in here!" She repeated, angrily.

They said nothing. She only heard breathing, heavy laborious horse-like breathing. She peered through the thin space between the door and the hinges to catch a glimpse of this person. But what she saw stole her breath away. Looking through the thin slot of open space was a blazing blue eye, wide as a gaping wound, staring back at her as if waiting.

She flinched backward onto the toilet with a small yelp, her heart racing as the eye continued to stare murderously at her.

For a moment, the two of them merely stared at each other, both panting like dogs. Only she panted out of fear whereas this person—this unblinking voyeur—panted like they were masturbating.

Then, the eye slide to the side out of her vision. And for a second, it was silent. Then, suddenly, the door shook violently. Fizzy leaped from her porcelain seat, her heart racing with wild fear, and slammed her body into the door like a rugby player. But the door shook harder and harder. She screamed for help, convinced she was going to be raped, but no sooner had she cried out loud than the shaking stopped. She didn't even realize the shaking had stopped until her entire body fell out of the stall and she landed on her shoulder, hard, against the tiled floors. She looked around and under every door, expecting to catch them, only to find herself alone in an empty bathroom.

"Jesus butt-fucking Christ," she murmured, thinking this was all merely a mean-spirited prank perpetrated by some pervert.

4.

She jogged out of the store, hoping the cold winter winds would stifle the aches in her chest. No sooner had she stepped out into the icy world than she felt her phone pulsate in her apron pocket. "Whaddup?"

"Sup bighead. When you get out of work?" asked Lonnie's canyon of a voice casually.

"Who you calling 'bighead'?" she replied, using a brick corner to shield herself from a freezing breeze.

"You! With your onion dome-shaped head."

"Bitch, you look like—and smell like—a bag of old onions."

"At least my forehead isn't big enough to be invaded by the US army."

Fizzy snickered, bested. "I get out at noon."

"Noon?!" It hadn't turned eight yet. "Those assholes aren't going to let you home after you told them your grandmother just died?"

Fizzy scoffed derisively. "I'm not wasting my personal time "grieving" over Jeanette Sobriquet."

"They should be giving you bereavement!" Tranquila's voice interjected from the nearby distance. "Your grandmother just got struck by fucking lightning, for fuck's sake."

"We even got a news link to prove it too if they try to give you shit for it," Lonnie assured.

"Send me that link immediately...but also, from the bottom of my heart, fuck that witch. I'd rather work the rest of my shift then pretend to give the slightest hint of a fuck about that soulless cun—"

Lonnie made a loud disparaging noise with her throat. "YEUGH! That's the dumbest shit I've ever heard you utter, sis. Also, look."

HONK! She turned her head and to her delighted surprise, Lonnie's clanky plastic silver steed pulled alongside the no parking zone. "Whaddup nerds!"

The passenger window rolled out and revealed her siblings: her green-haired, bronzer-obsessed teenage sister and her curly-headed, freckled-faced twenty-something brunet brother.

"What?" she said blankly as both her younger siblings mean-mugged her.

"You're really going to choose to work the rest of your shift just to be spiteful," Lonnie asked without amusement, "Over swallowing your pride, faking a few tears, and getting some sweet paid leave?"

"Ye-up," said Fizzy. But then she stopped, seized by her own stupidity. "Wait—what am I saying? Ugh. Give me ten minutes."

Her siblings' proud cheers followed her through the automatic doors.

"Hey," she said to her manager as they hunched over a quarter sheet cake. "My grandmother died. So, I need the weekend off for—"

"Go to Hell."

She balked mid-sentence. They hadn't even turned their head. "I'm being serious." She started to reach for her phone, saying, "She got struck by lightning…"

But her manager cut her off, eyes focused on the sugary project before them. "I'm being serious too. You didn't give forty-eight hours' notice."

"How the hell was I supposed to predict my grandmother getting—struck—by—lightning?" A blinding rage overflooded her and before she could stop herself, she watched herself ball up her apron, heave it to the ground and tell her boss of six years exactly how to fuck off, and ran out the door.

"So, did they give you the weekend off?" Lonnie asked as she ran over to his car.

"No, but it doesn't matter anyway because I quit my job."

"What?!" her siblings blurted out.

"Yeah...I should probably get my car off the property ASAP cause I one hundred percent said some shit I shouldn't have. I'll meet you guys at my place!" She told them quickly before making a shame-filled dash to her car.

Lonnie and Tranquila looked at each other then shook their heads in exasperation.

5.

When she left the parking lot, the dull gelid March
sun shined down on her. The drive home was magnificent.
The sun's rays magnified in her windshield, turning her
rusted-to-shit mobile into a mini sauna as if a gesture of
condolences.

She was halfway home when her best friend's
contact photo flashed across her phone. She tapped on the
speaker immediately and greeted her with an affectionate,
"Sup slut?"

"Oh my god, wanna hear the funniest story?"
Zeno's easy-breezy summertime voice cried out jovially
from the other line.

"Duh."

"Okay so I'm at work and I have to interpret for this
one guy, right? Old ass dude and he brought in his old ass

wife and I go in and of course, I know them, right? Turns out our families knew each other; they knew my grandma back in the old country; I used to be friends with their granddaughter back in elementary school—blah blah blah, anyway we're all catching up, joking. Finally, the doctor comes in and they're like 'your test results show you have Gonorrhea'. So, mind you, I have to tell this decrepit ass man he's got an S-T-D, in front of his equally dusty ass wife. And I relay the message and oh my god—this woman just loses her shit, INSTANTLY! She's all screaming at him in Bosnian and I'm sitting there trying not to laugh my ass off while the doctor's just sitting there looking scared shitless."

"No!"

"Wait—it gets better!"

"Oh my god. Please continue."

"So anyway, this lady's screaming her fucking head off and she's just like 'you fucking pig, da da da, you whore! I can't believe this! I can't even look at you! What do you have to say for yourself?' And, this dude—the fucking audacity of men, I swear—he looks her dead in the face and goes 'I can't help it! You know I'm addicted to the pussy'."

Fizzy let out a shocked gasp of a laugh. "The steel balls on that one!"

"Right?!" Zeno laughed. "But yeah, let me tell you, I've never seen an old lady sucker punch an old man in the nuts before but I'm glad I can say I checked that off my bucket list today."

Fizzy belly-laughed. "Damn, sounds like we both had interesting mornings."

"Why, what happened to you?"

"Well, I quit my job."

"What?! Why?!"

"Because I tried asking for the weekend off so I could go to my grandma's funeral and they told me to fuck off so I told them to fuck off and now they're going to be hella fucked because they're down two whole employees right before the weekend and I couldn't be happier," Fizzy replied with a vindictive laugh.

"Damn, Fizz. You give zero fucks." Zeno replied. "Also, your grandma died and you weren't going to tell me?!"

"Bitch, what do you think I'm doing now?"

"Awww…I'm sorry, Fizz. I didn't even know your dad's mom was still alive."

"She's not. I'm talking about Jeanette."

49

"That bitch is dead?!" Zeno blurted out in disbelief after a short stretch of stunned silence followed. "Like, dead-dead?!"

"Apparently," Fizzy said, her voice unreadable. Zeno strained to hear something in her voice. Anger, sadness, regret. Something. "Although I'm not believing shit until I see the body."

Her voice dropped to that of a murmur. "Wow."

"Yeah…"

Zeno paused then asked, tenderly, "How are you doing, Fizz?"

"Good." She said quickly. "I was thinking of having a deathday party tonight."

Her cavalier did not shock Zeno. Jeanette's death was an often talked about subject for Fizzy: how she doubted she'd ever see the day ("She'll outlive us all out of spite.") but, if by some miracle it ever did happen, she'd throw the biggest party to commemorate it. What worried Zeno was the nothingness in Fizzy's tone.

"What time? I work at *Dunkin* til six."

"I don't know. I was thinking nine." She informed. "Figured I'd have a couple of people over, play some beer pong ball and make some chicken wing dip. Nothing wild-wild."

Zeno chuckled. "I'm shocked your family isn't throwing that big ass block party y'all always talked about."

"Eh. Maybe after the funeral." She paused and when she spoke again, Zeno could hear the curl in her lips forming, "So...I was thinking of inviting Joanna."

Zeno made a noise she wasn't proud of: something between a delirious squawk and a squeal of lechery. She made that sound a lot at the mention of Joanna and it never failed to make Fizzy laugh.

"God, you're worse than a cat in heat!" Fizzy remarked good-naturedly.

"Shut up!" Zeno snapped. "Also, I love you and I can't wait to see you later and hug you and celebrate that wicked witch's death."

"I love you too, Zenny." She said as she pulled into the driveway of the crooked duplex where they both lived. "I gotta go though. I'll see you later."

"Good luck, Fizzy," Zeno said with a feminine endearment. "Love ya."

"I love you too." She said before she tapped the conversation to an end, looked out her window, and watched as her brother's car pulled alongside her own. She tore her messy fire red hair out of its sweaty bun, fixed her sweat-soaked bangs until they hide her forehead full of acne, turned her car off then go out and approached her brother's window.

"Mom wants to talk to you," Lonnie informed.

Fizzy let out a long, beleaguered sigh. She saw what would happen should she go to her mother's like a premonition. "She's just going to guilt me slash yell at me into going to the funeral."

Lonnie and Tranquila frowned, confirming her statement.

"Dude, it's two hours out of your life." Tranquila plead. "Three most."

"And we'll be higher than astronaut titties the whole time," Lonnie added.

Fizzy frowned, hard. "How can you…?" She stopped then started again, her blue-orange eyes narrowed. "After all that woman put us through. After all, that woman did to mom!"

"We're not doing this for her," Lonnie interrupted. "We're doing this for mom."

"Okay, but who screwed over mom the most in her life? Jeanette."

"We—" Lonnie began but Fizzy ranted over him.

"Who set mom's hair on fire during a friendly game of *UNO*? Jeanette." To Lonnie, she demanded, "Who stole your identity AND almost framed you for treason? *Jeanette*." To Tranquila, she said, "Who tricked you into selling your soul to Hades just because she was bored? JEANETTE. Who—"

"You don't have to remind us that grandma was a piece of shit," Tranquila said. "We already know."

"So why honor her at all by going to her funeral?"

"Because it was her last wish," Lonnie said. Fizzy bent down to see her brother bear a look of resignation that broke her heart. "It was her final wish that all her family goes to her funeral. And mom wants to respect her final wishes."

"Sounds like a not-my-problem," Fizzy said with the finality of someone who was done with a tiresome conversation. Lonnie and Tranquila tried to talk but she cut them off with, "Fuck that! I'm not going to that woman's funeral or her wake, or her memorial, or her whatever the fuck she's got set up for herself."

"Fizz..." Lonnie began but she had already turned towards her home.

"Tell mom I'm sorry. I know this is the last thing she wants in the world right now and I know I probably seem like the biggest bitch in the world right now but I can't go to that funeral and pretend to give an honest fuck about that: loathsome, vile, vindictive, child-abusing, degenerate-gambling, controlling super bitch." Fizzy vowed as she trampled up the crooked dingy yellow steps leading to her front door. "Also, I'm throwing a party tonight to celebrate that bitch's death. You guys are welcome to come and smoke mad blunts with me if you choose. But only if you want to. Love you both."

With that, she disappeared, leaving her siblings to sit silently in the idling car.

"It's only Wednesday," Lonnie said softly. "She's got time to change her mind."

Tranquila frowned, saying nothing with a look on her face that bespoke quiet, growing dread.

When Fizzy got inside her piss-yellow apartment and plopped herself in front of her bong, she discovered she had six additional missed calls from her mother. She ignored them all in favor of indulging in a slow, skunky paradise.

By the inky evening, a third car pulled into the driveway of 1215 Carter Street. A voluptuous, olive-skinned white woman with brownie-battered hair tied into a tall knot above her square-faced head and a smile that could chip an iceberg emerged from her coworker's car, sipping on an iced coffee despite the flurries that swirled around her. She thanked her coworker with cash and hurried up the crooked ear-wax yellow porch steps where a fat, elderly brown man in a dozen layers smoked a corncob pipe.

"Hey Grandpa Claus," she greeted as she searched her winter coat for her house key.

"Red blue Rudolph busy this year," he remarked casually, eyes locked on the drifts of snow that came down from cloud-covered heavens, in a warbled, garbled voice that made him sound like he was trying to speak underwater.

Translation: "The temperature's supposed to get into the negatives."

"That's what I heard," she replied, shivering. She wanted to bolt inside but steeled her body against the cold as she turned to face him. She could never end a conversation with the elderly first.

"You (incoherent) hop wallet... in (incoherent) Sherlock's salad spinner?"

Translation: "I hope your roommate put enough gas in her car. It'll freeze in the tank if she didn't."

55

"I'll let her know either way," she promised, her bare, heavily inked hands shaking as she fumbled for the right key.

He made a 'hmmph' noise with his mouth, his cracked lips curled around the end of his pipe, looking suddenly engrossed with thoughts, ending their friendly chat.

She shoved her key into the lock and opened the second door. She hopped over the threshold, crying out a goodbye to Grandpa Claus before she sealed herself into the weed-smelling stairwell. She darted up the two flights of stairs and emerged into the living room to find her best friend of sixteen years, eyes as red as the cystic acne that scrawled her jawline, looking stuck within a self-made haze.

"It's brick titties out there!" Zeno announced, kicking off her snow caked boots. "I heard it's supposed to get into the negatives tonight."

"Ugh! I knew I forgot to do something before I got home." Fizzy groaned, tossing her head back into the couch. Then she picked her head up and asked, "Wanna go on a trip with me to the gas station later?"

"No."

"C' mon…I'll buy you a beef patty."

56

"Okay." Zeno shrugged off her coat, hung it on a loose nail, and hopped onto the unoccupied couch opposing Fizzy with the relieved sigh of someone who got to sit for the first time in eight hours. She watched Fizzy reach for her blue and white glass bong and pack the stem with ground-up weed before she asked, "How you doing, Fizz?"

"I'm great. My worst enemy is finally dead, it's payday, I got to tell a boss to fuck off for the first time in my entire life AND I don't have to work tomorrow. So. I. Am. Great."

But Zeno, unconvinced, got off the couch and crossed over to the loveseat to embrace Fizzy, who squeezed Zeno for half-a-minute in grateful silence. When they pulled away from each other, they discovered they were both crying. For a moment, they were nothing but embarrassed giggles and relieved tears.

6.

Affidious had no sooner gotten home after dropping Olivia off to work, intending to go straight to bed and catch a few more hours of sleep before work, when his phone went off. He glanced at the screen and let out an irritated groan when he saw the contact name TITS pop up.

"This better be important. You know how I feel about conversing when the sun is still out." He said as soon as he answered the call with a yawn.

"I know, I know," began his old friend, "but this is important. I got a letter here for you that says 'do not leave in mailbox. Give to the recipient immediately'. In big red letters and everything."

"Just leave it in my mailbox," Affidious insisted in-between a more powerful yawn.

"Okay, player. Oh, also, I thought you should know, there's a shady-looking white dude just standing outside the bar."

"Man, tell that cracker to kick rocks." He replied. "Until we open at six, then he's welcomed back to come and spend his money."

"I did but he just ignored me." Then a sound came out of Tits that Affidious, in his many years of knowing the man, had never heard before. He shuddered. "You should probably get down here. There's something about this motherfucker I do not trust."

Without missing a beat, Affidious turned his car back on and told Tits, "I'm on my way."

Five failed businesses gathered on the same block as *the Topspin*, huddled together like the fuck-ups at a family reunion. Their windows were black, their doors were nailed shut, and litter splattered the ground like vomit. Yet, there thrived *the Topspin*.

Affidious spotted the man's car before anything, mostly because the man in question parked like an asshole: Slanted, tail-end sticking out into the road as if waiting for someone to rear-end them, in front of not only a fire hydrant but a sign that specifically said 'no parking on this side'. Then he glanced at his bar and saw the white man standing on the sidewalk, his pasty white head shining against the astringent sun, still as a statue, his hands dug into his jean pockets.

The white man caught Affidious' gaze and held it as the car crawled and eventually stopped alongside the ice-blanched roads. When he got out of the car, the white man's blazing dead man's blue eyes were still locked onto him with an impassive expression.

The two of them continued their staring contest for a few seconds before Affidious threw his thick arms to his sides and demanded, "You got a problem?"

The white man said nothing but he wore an expression of vague disdain. As if he was being the weirdo, standing in front of a closed bar in the middle of March with only a thin army light brown jacket on, no hat to cover his bald head or gloves for his bluish hands despite the freezing temperature.

Affidious gave him another hard look before he trekked over to the parked mail truck sitting idling in front of his bar.

"Hey man," greeted Tits without enthusiasm.

"Hey. How long has he been there?"

"Since before I got here." Tits replied as he handed him his mail. The two of them looked over and saw the stranger was observing them. He let out another shudder then told Affidious, "Ugh, have fun dealing with that."

They gave each other dab then parted ways.

Affidious turned and found the stranger's unwavering stares zeroed in on him. But Affidious was fearless by force of will and thus when he went to the front door of *the Topspin,* he told the white man as he passed by, like an afterthought, "We're not open yet."

The man said nothing and Affidious studied the man's face for a second. It occurred to him at that moment that this man might be Bosnian—he glanced at the man's car and a blue and yellow miniature flag hanging from his mirror confirmed his theory—and that he must not know English, and that's why he didn't respond to Tits nor him when he spoke.

"Not. O-pen." Affidious repeated slowly before he turned back to the bar and began the process of fumbling for the right key. He hadn't taken four steps up the stoop when he became aware of a presence following him. When he looked over his shoulder the foreigner stood at the bottom of the step as if waiting to be let in. Affidious let out a frustrated growl, then pointed to the sign that bore the bar's operating hours. He pointed to Wednesday's hours 6 pm to 2 am and reiterated they were not open.

The stranger didn't even blink. He merely stared at him with those terrible blue eyes. *A shade darker than a dead man's eyes*, Affidious thought although in his head the voice sounded more like his mother's (he never noticed until then how his more poetic thoughts always sounded like something Olivia would say).

A freezing wind passed through him, slicing him to the bone, and Affidious felt himself getting more and more irritated with this man. He shuffled the stack of mail into one hand and used his free hand to point to the road, shouting as he did, "GO!"

But the man continued to stare at him with slow-to-blink eyes and the same, disinterested expression instilled on his pale face.

Fed up, Affidious started down the steps. He planned to intimidate the man with his stature, for he was a few inches taller, much wider, and darker, than the loiterer. But no sooner had he started towards the man did he reach into his jacket pocket and pull out a handgun.

Affidious stilled instantly on that step, his left foot receding backward as he slowly raised his hands to his shoulders. For a few horrible seconds, neither of them moved or spoke. They simply stared at the other: the white man with his blazing eyes steeled on Affidious and Affidious' gaze locked on the gun that was pointed at his stomach.

The world around him slowed until every second stretched out before him like a rubber band. He saw his death, no—*he felt Death*—standing behind him, hovering so close he could hear Its guttural breath brush against the nylon of his winter coat.

This is it, he thought despairingly as the gun gleamed underneath the end of Winter sun. *I'm going to die. I'm going to get gunned down in front of my own bar, in the broad daylight. All that yoga and oatmeal for nothing...*

Then, the gunman made a gesture with his weapon that Affidious, in his wild fear, didn't understand right away. Noticing the incomprehension in his eyes, the gunman gestured again to the door.

Oh, Affidious realized finally, *this is just a stick-up.*

He held up his keys, raising his eyebrows quizzically as he did and the white man gave him an impatient nod. Shaky Affidious unlocked the door, raised his hands back to his shoulders, and slowly lead them inside the bar.

The gunman followed him inside and closed the door behind him with his foot, sealing them into whatever fate he had in store for him. Affidious eyed the gun as he waited for the stranger to give him further instructions.

But the white man didn't say a word. Instead, Affidious watched as he slid into the nearest booth, the barrel of his gun never straying from Affidious' person, and made himself comfortable.

Affidious waited while the man took his time, terrified that one wrong move would be fatal, but the blue-eyed stranger didn't seem interested in him anymore. His focus had turned onto the bar, which he regarded with unsmiling silence. Affidious watched him as his head swiveled this way and that, taking in the wall of photos, the pool table, the stools, the decorations, and the shelves of booze.

He did this for an uncomfortably long time. Affidious was convinced this was a power move. A way of making him sweat out his last few minutes of life.

Affidious cleared his throat. When the man looked his way, he nodded towards the cash register.

But the man with the gun shook his head.

So, this isn't a stick-up? He wondered, bewildered. *Why is he here then?*

As if reading his thoughts, the blue-eyed man placed the gun on the table then used his hands to mime. He held his hands in front of him, then lowered his eyes to his palms, his face scrunched with thought.

Affidious had no fucking clue what any of that meant and when the man noticed this, he let out a loud irritated sigh then pointed to Affidious' hand. Affidious looked down and discovered he still had today's mail in his hand. He gave the man a confused look. It wasn't until he did the same gesture again that it hit Affidious.

"You want me to read my mail?" He asked, flummoxed.

The man wagged his hairless chin at him affirmatively.

Affidious looked at the mail, then at the strange man, then back at the mail. Most of it was junk—flyers, coupons to places he didn't shop at, a jury duty questionnaire he had no intention of filling out—but he held them up individually to the white man who shook his head at each of them. Then, finally, he flipped to a thick, off-white envelope which beheld in giant red letters URGENT DO NOT LEAVE IN MAILBOX GIVE TO RECIPIENT IMMEDIATELY and bore the logo to an attorney's office he didn't recognize. When he held it up to the white man, he nodded and gestured at him, his thumb and index finger pointed at him like a gun, to open it.

What the fuck is going on, he thought but said nothing as he tore open the letter.

He brandished the letter to the white man, assuming he wanted to read it, but the white man shook his head and pointed his chin to him. As if to say, *read it*.

He looked at the letter, then back to him, then back to the letter and began to read.

7.

He read aloud:

"Dear Fiddy,

"If you're reading this, that means I am dead. As such, I am calling in on that favor you owe me.

"I'm not asking for a lot. I know you have your hands full running the bar and taking care of that mother of yours. But it is this humble" (he sneered at the word knowing she never knew the meaning) *"woman's last wish for her entire family to be at her funeral. It's my only wish and I'm asking you, as a friend, to please make sure they all"* ('all' was underlined three times) *"go."*

Damn, Jeanette, you can never leave them be? Even in the afterlife? He thought.

"Lucky for you I have a small family: My daughter, Darlene Sobriquet, and my grandchildren, Lonnie Obiit

67

Odette Obiit and Tranquila Obiit are all that remains of me
in this mortal coil. Out of all of them, the only one I know
for certain is going to give you a hard time about not going
is Odette. (See photo attached)." He turned over the letter
and found a printout of a selfie. A young white woman in a
face full of makeup with scarlet flat-ironed shoulder-length
hair, small blue-orange eyes, and a large, crooked nose
gave him a chubby-lipped smile. He flipped the photo over
and was disgusted to see information about her scribbled
into the back: Where she lived and worked; the phone
numbers to both jobs; her best friend's name and
information; her car's make, model, and license plate. He
turned the photo over and stared at the young woman with
small pity, thinking, *Shit, I'd skip the funeral too if I were*
you.

     "I ask that you make sure that she attends my
funeral, which will be held at Sugi Pula's Funeral Home *on*
Saturday at 9 am. It is my only request and I hope that out
of respect to me you will do me this favor. Ha hahaha.

     "All jokes aside, see that bald man sitting in the
booth next to the door with the gun? That man is a friend of
mine." Affidious glanced up over the stationary to catch the
man's unsmiling stares. Fresh fear slowly congealed his
blood as he continued to read, *"Back in Bosnia, he was*

known as the Wraith. Because every time you saw that motherfucker you knew either you or someone you loved was going to die or already had died. He has agreed, as a favor to me, to make sure that you make due on your favor to me. If you do not fulfill my last request, he has been instructed to kill Dr. Olivia Dixon. Although trust me when I say, murder will be the kindest thing he does to her. Ha hahaha.

"You have four days (well, minus tonight of course. We all know how busy Wednesday nights are for you ☺).
Anyway, good luck! I'm rooting for you Fiddy!

"Sincerely,

"Your fucked-up fairy godmother.

"P.S. Think I'm fucking with you? Google him, dickfuck."

He re-read the last paragraph with a shallow, ragged breath. When he looked up at the Wraith, his entire body pulsating with terror, the man gave him a sly, brazen wink.

No, he thought as he dug into his pocket to retrieve his phone convinced that this was all a cruel, sick joke (not without reason too. Jeanette loved cruel, sick jokes). But a quick Google search told him everything he needed to know about the man sitting in the booth with the gun pointed at his belly: His name, his early life, his role in the Bosnian genocide, and how back in 2001 the UN charged him with, among other things:

1.Multiple counts of torture, rape, and enslavement of Bosnian Muslim females in 1992.

2. The repeated beatings, tortures, and mass executions of Bosnian Muslim males in 1992

3. The inhumane treatment and/ or torture of Bosnian Muslims, Bosnian Croats, and other non-Serbs— including beatings, tortures, sexual violence, and death threats in 1992.

4. One count of genocide.

Reading the litany of atrocities made his blood freeze but what seized his heart with unmitigated terror was when he got to the end of the search and saw a link to a video of the man before him avoiding jail time by drinking poison—back in 2001.

Affidious looked up at the Wraith then back at his phone then back at the Wraith again. *No*, he thought. *No. This is bullshit…*

As if reading his thoughts, the Wraith gave him a cruel smile. One that was desperate for depravity.

Without thinking, Affidious chucked his phone at the Wraith but the phone flew through the man as if he didn't exist and shattered against the brick wall with a heart-stopping thud. Affidious trembled silently as the coffee he had that morning gushed onto the floor.

8.

The Wraith waited until the very last driblet of piss hit the ground before he slid out from underneath the booth, stuffed his gun into his jacket, and told Affidious, in a voice as deep and gentle as the ocean, "Vidimose."

Then, without saying another word, he left.

Affidious waited until he heard his footfalls fade away before he ran to the window facing the street. He hoped to catch the Wraith's license plate but when he made it to the window, nearly slipping in the puddle of urine he left, twice, the car was gone and so was the Wraith. Not even tire tracks remained.

9.

Affidious mopped up his mess, then walked back to his car, his thick neck tucked into his coat and his shoulders squared, his eyes squinted protectively against the sharp, blade-like wind. Once he was within the confines of his car, did his body tense again, only this time with an unending rage. That is when he let out the world's longest, "Fuuuuuuuuuuuuuuuuuuuuuuuuuuuuuuuuuuuuuuuuuuuuuuuuu uuuuuuuuuuuuuuuuuuuuuuuuuuuck!"

10.

After he changed his pants, got a new phone,
activated it, gave everyone in his contacts the new number,
picked his mother up from work, and watched her take her
afternoon medications, Affidious spent the rest of his day
leading into the night cruising around town. He went down
busy roads, waded through rush hour with his radio off, his
head turning every way, scanning the darkness. The first
few he saw were women, bundled in dirty coats, unkempt
hair jammed underneath knitted hats, some standing alone,
others with children against their thighs, standing
underneath no panhandling signs with signs of their own:
'Anything helps' 'God bless' 'Hungry'.

Ugh, he thought as he sped past them, too
depressing.

He went the long way downtown, leaning left and right hoping to catch the sight of a grocery cart full of cans pushed by some ramshackle drunk. But he coasted along and saw only sealed up tents.

He tried to ignore the digitalized thermometer that glowed inside his dashboard telling him it was below freezing but the worry came anyway.

What if tonight wasn't going to happen?

He shook that thought away and as soon as he did—bam.

A skinny brown kid, with a face that made him look young and old all at once, stepped in front of his headlight brandishing a sign: Will Work for Food/ $

He had three face tattoos, faded red hair like a burgeoning sunset, he wore a cheap leather jacket with a blue flannel hoodie underneath and a tattered pair of red flannel pajama bottoms, he had a loose cigarette tucked between his beanie.

Affidious rolled down his window and harked, "Hey! I got work if you're interested."

The homeless homie didn't move at first until Affidious flashed a folded-up bill. Then, he stuffed the sign into his backpack, threw it over his shoulder then meandered over, hands jammed into his pockets, shoulders squared against the horrible wind. "What kind of work?"

"I work at a bar. One of my workers called in and I got a delivery of beer coming in tonight." He explained. "It'd be an hour of work, tops."

His legs shook while he thought. "How much?"

"Fiddy bucks."

He pondered some more, but for less time. "Is it far from here?"

"A little. About a mile." Affidious offered, slowly stretching his hand out for the man.

The homeless homie took the money then rounded the front of the car. "Thanks, man." He said as he closed the passenger door.

"No, thank YOU, man." Affidious insisted as he yanked his car into drive. "You're doing me a huge favor."

In the six-minute drive back to *the Topspin*, the homeless homie managed to thank him no less than fifteen times. He also managed to tell him the truncated version of his entire life story: How he'd been on the streets since he ran away from home from his abusive family at 15; how he got diagnosed with bipolar and PTSD; how he used to work—and oh how he insisted that he wasn't a bum—he just got hurt bad and the medical bills kept billing up and no matter how much money he made the hospitals would take it all anyway; how long he'd been standing there all night praying to God for someone like him to come his way. He talked about the baby he badly missed and then he swore, up and down, how he wasn't on drugs, honest, even though everyone thought he was. Then he talked about the woman who tried to run him over the other day, screaming horrible things about how he was making the city look bad by begging for money. And then he cried a little and thanked him again then went on about the documentary he was thinking of filming, on his flip phone, about his life.

"You should," Affidious said once he pulled past *the Topspin*, rolling over the dirty-snow-covered lot where deep tracks marks of where delivery trucks came and went ran beside an over-flowing dumpster.

"You think so?"

"Absolutely." He replied as he turned the car off. "This is it."

"I think I'm gonna." The homeless homie said. He took him by the sleeve, looked him in the eyes, and said, "Thank you. You have no idea…I prayed for an angel like you to show up in my life."

Affidious clasped his hand onto the man's and said, "You don't have to thank me. I'm just doing what I think is right." Then they exited the car.

Affidious went ahead up a small set of concrete stairs that lead to a loading dock. Affidious used his key to unlock a metal door that blended into the back of the bar. "We can wait inside while the truck comes."

He led them up a dark stairwell using the bluish light from his phone, taking two steps at a time until they hit a second closed-door underneath a beaming exit sign. Affidious opened the door for his companion who slid by and was greeted by the warm, welcoming babbling of a busy bar. Patrons looked up from their drinking and paused their conversing to greet Affidious like a celebrity.

"What's your name again?" Affidious asked as he went behind the bar to gather empty bottles and replenish empty glasses.

"Travis."

"Hey everyone!" Affidious hollered, drawing the attention of his customers. "Travis, here, is helping me with delivery!"

The room erupted with cheers. One man who sat at the counter, fiddling with a tv remote, thanked him by name. Travis stood there, awkward but heartened.

"You're doing me a huge favor," Affidious' voice told him as half of him disappeared into a walk-in cooler.

He returned with a water bottle and handed it to Travis who took it with a grateful nod. His phone went off and he cursed when he read the message.

"Damn. The driver's already here. Would you mind meeting them?" Affidious asked. "I gotta serve these assholes first."

"No problem." He tucked the water bottle into his coat pocket, slid his bookbag off his shoulders, and stashed the tattered bag underneath the bar, in-between the garbage can and a digitalized safe.

"Thanks again, Travis." The name rolled off his tongue as if it belonged to a dear friend. "I can't thank you enough."

His head was down, focused on the register as Travis departed for the backdoor, but he watched him from the corner of his eye, waiting for him to get to the stairwell. The second the man's foot touched the metal threshold, he gave a quick nod and without hesitation, one of the patrons got up from their stool and followed Travis to the door.

Travis didn't hear the other man's footsteps over the hustle of the bar. He was already going down the first set of concrete steps when his ears noticed the bewildering sound of the second pair of footfalls. Then, the unmistakable sound of a heavy door coming to close.

He spun around in the darkness, to run towards the door, only to hear the gears of a lock sealing him within the concrete catacomb.

He tripped trying to run back up the steps, falling hard on his chin. His top set of teeth bashed against the lower lip and he tasted blood. He reached for his face, tenderly, letting out a small cry as he felt for a cut but then panic sent him upright. He swung his arms around in search of the railing and when he found the thing, he clamored to it for dear life with both hands, his legs quivering, his balance thrown off from the total darkness, his heart racing as visceral terror swept through him and the sounds of laughter echoed from behind the closed door.

They watched the struggle in night vision mode from Affidious' laptop, throwing money at the barkeep as Travis screamed.

A whiteboard hung above the liquor license that read two things: First read, Cover Charge $250. The second was odds for those who wanted a little side action:

2 to 1 said he'll die in 5 seconds or less

2 to 5 said he won't see it coming

10 to 1 said he'd surprise them by fighting for his life, using a weapon they weren't aware of, a knife or, maybe if they were lucky, a gun.

1000 to 1 said he'd make it out alive but that was a ridiculous bet. Everyone knew no one got out alive when PJ was nearby.

Affidious stood by with a pen and pad, jotting down the bets as they came. And oh, how the bets poured in. They crowded him, shouting over another furiously. For the rule went, they only had until the demon made his presence known to place their wages.

Then, came the growl. The low, threatening, rumble like thunder roaring directly overhead. And then the whole bar went silent as they pushed another to get a better spot behind the glowing screen.

Affidious tucked the currency into his apron and turned the laptop towards him without opposition. The patrons crowded around him their eyes peeled and their mouths slack with bloodlust.

Travis made it to the door and they watched him as he pounded the metal door feebly, his balled-up fists so small and ridiculous on the screen. He shouted for clemency with only garnered jeers from the crowd. No one likes a coward.

Then, the growl came again and they cheered as they watched a shadowy figure thrice Travis's height draws up the stairs. Its heavy footfalls ricocheted off the blackened walls like cannons. They watched Travis start to tremble, some shouting at the screen demands to run, to fight, to turn around, to look in the face of his doom, and be braver than they ever would.

But Travis did something most men did when they realized death was behind them hungry, hate-filled, and devoid of clemency.

For as the giant creature unhinged its deformed jaw and unleashed a roar that shook even Affidious to his core, to this very day, Travis screamed for divine mercy. But his head was ripped off his shoulders before he discovered too late that the Gods weren't concerned.

PART TWO: VIDIMOSE*

*Bosnian: "See you later"

1.

Fizzy ignored her screeching phone, which told her
when she checked later that she had now ten missed calls
and eight four-minute-long voicemails from her mom, and
went through her skincare routine. Her blue-orange eyes
darting side to side, up and down, to spare herself from
ruining her day. She tried like hell to avoid being depressed
the day before, or day of, her weekends, preferring to delay
it on her workdays when she usually was depressed
anyway. She did this because even glancing at her bare face
walloped her down a pit that made it impossible to leave
the duplex let alone make money and not starve.

Her skin was like a cluster of fire ants climbing over
a field of eggshells, conquering both cheeks, her chin, and
her forehead. No matter the products she bought, the
dermatologists she visited, the effort she put day and night

into rectifying her genetic tragedy, the angry red acne remained.

Outside her room laid a hallway where Zeno's bedroom and their bathroom stood. Beyond that were a near-vertical flight of stairs which led to the living room/kitchen and a slightly larger second bathroom where a floor-length mirror and a broken washing machine were kept. On the broken washing machine sat a small circular, dual-sided mirror with a string of white lights tapped around the frame. Inside the broken dryer was a treasure trove of makeup bags, so many, with so many designs and colors, it looked like a cubby for the beauty-obsessed.

Literal thousands of dollars were hidden in that dryer and because she was a hot mess who feared the covetousness of others, she kept them hidden. Five times a week she would rifle through the makeup bags, cherry-picking through the vast assortments of beautifiers like an artist deliberates which medium to create with that day. Her amassed makeup was more expensive than oils and canvases. If Da Vinci was alive today, he would've no doubt been in awe of her collection. Unlike him, she could wear her art, carry it everywhere she went, unlike him or Artemisia Gentileschi or Edmonia Lewis, whose work was snatched up by museums and left to collect dust in spaces most people would never see. While hers garnered no money or fame, she carried her art to the public and kept it for herself. No one would try to snatch hers or smuggle it, forge it, hoard it, hide it, pass it off as their own.

A few of their walls, too, bore her art. Whenever her makeup would expire, the idea of shucking them into the trash offended her deeply. So, instead of clogging landfills, she'd buy a small canvas—cheap ones from a discount store that 200 years ago would've taken weeks to procure—and transfer gunky foundations, lipsticks, and pore-clogging eyeshadows onto them. Her art pieces were plastered throughout the apartment.

She sat on her repurposed chair and began the first of many steps into making her skin not hideous.

She started by draining two dollars' worth of liquid skin onto a pink egg-shaped sponge, smoothing the excess with the back of her hand and dabbing her cheeks, forehead, under-eyes, and chin until the little volcanos that scarred her face were smoothed into a sea of creamy magma.

Within forty minutes she sculpted a new face for herself—a flawless countenance that would've made Botticelli puke from jealousy with her talent and speed. She went through all of this, five days a week, not for the world to fall in love with her but just so she could walk out the door and not seethe in self-loathing the entire time.

The best kind of parties in life are a) spontaneous and b) the ones you barely remember. Birthday parties and costume parties are close seconds. Deathday parties are probably dead last but that didn't prevent Fizzy from trying to turn her grandmother's death-day party into a banger.

Unfortunately, both her siblings bailed on principle. "It's not right to talk ill about the dead," said Tranquila solemnly.

To which Fizzy recited the only Voltaire quote she knew, "To the living, we owe respect but to the dead, we owe the truth."

By ten o'clock the tiny apartment was teeming with life. Fizzy was watching a lively game of beer pong in the kitchen, enjoying a blunt Zeno rolled for her, while the sounds of her friends screaming competitively at another filled her heart with unending joy. Sometimes she would catch herself smiling at her reflection, telling the clear-skinned woman in the kitchen window silently, *I feel like the happiest motherfucker that ever fucked.*

Then the sound of the door opening knocked her out of her reverie and she turned her head towards her best friend's ear and said in a singsong voice, "Guess who's here..."

Zeno's glossy eyes widened at once. She scanned the room but she didn't look far. Four steps from where she stood and all she had to do were catch sight of the heavily inked shaved-headed beauty that stole her heart. *Joanna*...her heart cooed. "Oh my god. Oh my god. Oh my god." She turned to Fizzy. "How do I look?"

"Beautiful, as always. Now go talk to her."

"No!"

Fizzy ignored her. She turned her neck to the couch where a dark brown woman in all black with a face full of metal and said, "Joanna, I wanna introduce you to somebody. This is my sister from another mister, Zeno, aka the honorary grandchild of the woman we're dishonoring tonight."

Joanna stood up at once. "Nice to meet you." Before she could say anything, Joanna held out her arms and asked, tentatively, "Are you a hugger?"

Oh my god, am I dead? Is this heaven? Is this the cool, gay heaven? Zeno thought as this beautiful, stocky, men's deodorant-smelling goddess wrapped her arms around her. When Joanna let go, Zeno was able to joke, "Thank you for the pity bear-hug."

"Oh my god, honey. No problem." Then to Fizzy, she said, "I'm so sorry for your loss, girl. I can only imagine what you and your family are going through right now." Joanna said, her thick hands laid against her chest empathetically. "I couldn't imagine if my grandma died tomorrow. Let alone got struck by lightning."

Fizzy took a tight drag from her blunt. "Oh yeah, it's a real loss." When she exhaled, she announced, "I'm going to go play beer pong." She turned her head over her shoulder and shouted, "Yo, Brynn! Wanna be my beer pong partner?"

"Does a rocking horse have a hickory dick?"

"Brynn, I fucking love you!" She laughed as they left to go into the kitchen to play against the winning team.

"Your best friend's...uh...taking it pretty hard, I can tell," Joanna commented.

"Well," Zeno said, "Not gonna lie, her grandma wasn't exactly the best person."

Joanna snorted a little, gesturing to a handmade banner strung above the TV that read, DING DONG THE BITCH IS DEAD. "I figured."

"Yeah, Fizzy fucking *hated* that woman." Zeno laughed, her voice dropping a full octave for emphasis. "But, in her defense, she has a lot of good reasons to."

"Hey, I'm not judging," Joanna said. "It says a lot more about her grandma than it does about her that she's this excited to see her gone." Then, she looked at her with a face that Zeno was both bewitched and faintly intimidated by. "What about you though? How do you feel about all this?"

Zeno barely heard the questions. She was too busy imagining their wedding day.

"Uh, what?" Zeno said snapping back into reality.

"Never mind," Joanna said with a laugh. Then she made a goofy smile that melted Zeno's heart instantly. "So, I gotta ask: Why do they call your friend Fizzy? Is it, like, an inside joke or is it because she's so bubbly?"

Zeno flashbacked to ninth grade, where she watched her best friend stick two straws up her nostrils, one plunged into a can of Pepsi, the other into a can of Cola, and snorted for a full 3.5 seconds before her nostrils nearly disintegrated and her world went white from carbonation overload just to win a money-less bet, a lifelong moniker and to be embarrassed every year whenever one of her former lunch table buddies reposted it on her social media timeline.

But like a good friend, she lied on Fizzy's behalf and said, "Oh, it's just something her mom always called her."

Fizzy glanced around her beer pong partner and beamed as the pair shared a conversation.

2.

Thursday

The apartment was quiet. The music had been turned off, the beer pong table is now folded up and stashed back underneath Fizzy's bed like the prized possession that it is and the downstairs is vacant of party-goers. All who remained were Zeno and Joanna, two dark-haired love birds, who pecked each other out on the loveseat.

After a few minutes of intense kissing, Joanna pulled herself from Zeno's face and asked, in a coy voice, "You tired?"

"No, actually I'm wide awake."

"Well…do you want to go upstairs anyway?"

By then, it was clear to Zeno this beauty was in no way sleepy. While a part of her did want to lead this cutie with the chest piece to her bedroom, she found herself inexplicably afraid. Like something bad would happen if she took her to the bedroom.

"I—I would but, these walls are so thin…and Fizzy's room is right next door to mine. I wouldn't be in the right mind space to fuck if I kept worrying about waking her ass up," she lied knowing damn well that after the ten blunts she smoked it would've taken a fire alarm and a good shove to wake Fizzy up.

Joanna gave her a look, a look that she recognized, with heart-stopping horror, could see through her feeble lies. "Okay."

An awkward, eye-avoidance silence ensued.

"You know, I'm gonna go…" Joanna announced as she stood up.

"No! I mean, you don't gotta…The night's so young."

"It's four am?"

"Yeah, like I said, it's still early," Zeno said. "We can go get breakfast…"

"I'm not hungry." She replied as she started to search for her car keys.

Zeno was so worried that, when she found those keys, she'd never see her again and that fear made her blurt out, "We can go on an adventure!"

Joanna had just found her keys underneath a throw pillow but the sound of the word 'adventure' made her delay her leave. "What kind of adventure?"

"Ever go ghost hunting during the Witching Hour?"

This made her right eye squint. "Where you had in mind?"

"I was thinking *the Topspin*," grinned Zeno, although inwardly she had no idea where the idea came from.

Joanna made a closed-mouth inhale. "You wanna go ghost hunting at the place where all those homeless people supposedly disappeared?" She stared at her as if torn between being afraid and being impressed. "That's the most macabre thing I've ever heard of."

"So…you're not down?"

"Fuck yeah I'm down!" Joanna said, the little goth teenager inside her all aflutter.

3.

Fizzy remembered being in a bar. It was late and she had a vague feeling telling her that she should be going somewhere, seeing someone. Then a male silvery voice came from the side.

"Hey, gorgeous. Can I buy you a drink?"

She turned her head and there stood a beautiful stranger with wavy brown hair, a strong jaw, and an ass to die for was leaning into the bar with a handsome devil's smile reserved only for her. Their conversation culminated when the stranger asked, in a voice so sweet, "Have you ever had your asshole licked by a man with a forked tongue before?" Seconds later they were in her childhood bed discovering each other's g-spots. Then the door flung open. Jeanette walked in wearing a wretched smile. She was covered in blood and she was making this horrendous sound, a savage laugh so cruel it paralyzed her with fear. "It's all your fault, Fizzy," Jeanette cried in a tinny sing-song voice. Fizzy had no idea what she meant until she saw Jeanette pull Zeno's severed head from behind her back. She watched in horror as Jeanette swung the bloodied head by a fist-full of brown locks around like a pendulum. The last thing she remembered was a bald man lying in the handsome stranger's place giving her a wink before he whispered in her ear, "Vidimose."

She jolted awake drenched in enough sweat to fill a sink. It took minutes for the tremors to cease but once her heart rate settled, she managed to push the image of Zeno's decapitated head from her mind and snatched a few more hours of sleep. By daylight, she forgot the dream entirely.

4.

Zeno borrowed Fizzy's car and took them both down to *the Topspin*, a bar over on Lincoln Avenue, the slums of the south side. *The Topspin*, a bar made out of so many bricks it fairly resembled one, and a giant 'NO TRESPASSING' sign which both ignored as Zeno tried to use the front door. It didn't work.

"C'mon," said Zeno, halfway down the front steps, "I know another way." She veered right, into a narrow alleyway, where they trampled on garbage and old needles to get to the backyard of the bar. They were greeted at once to the rank, nostril curling smell of a dumpster that hadn't been dumped in several years. Holding her shirt to her mouth, Joanna watched as Zeno ripped vines from the back of the bar, revealing, underneath, a metal door. To their joy, the door opened with a simple turn, leading to an entrance so black they both whipped out their phones to shine a light. But the eerie blue luminescence did not ease the clump of dread that formed in Joanna's stomach as they stepped inside and, with Zeno leading the way, went through a hollowed backway, up a flight of steps to another door with a broken exit sign hovering above it as if to say, 'watch where you step, little idiots.'

Zeno led them from the empty stairwell into a small corridor, which comprised of three doors, aged by neglect, cobwebs, and ugly chipped brown paint. She pointed to one of the doors.

She turned the doorknob. The door only made it two-thirds of the way open before it slammed against a giant filing cabinet. It was a cramped office space, no bigger than one of those bathrooms where it only possessed a toilet and a sink. Joanna thought of that as her eyes fell upon a sign that read 'a man's office is the best place to think—outside of Le Can'. The whole room, like the rest of the bar, smelled stale and stuffy. Zeno stepped inside and began rummaging through the desk, which had stacks of notebooks and receipt books everywhere. She chose to merely open and close each of the drawers.

Joanna scooched around Zeno to sit at the desk, in a fold-up chair whose cushion had long been worn down by overuse. When her butt made contact with his chair, something shocked her into leaping back to her feet. She yelped. "What's wrong?" Zeno asked but she didn't have an answer. Suddenly, all her fascination from earlier drained, and the sight of Zeno flipping through old notebooks made her nervous. Zeno wasn't even reading them, she was just letting her thumb rub against the yellowed pages, making one of her favorite sounds—that pffpffpff of written on papers—the sound of which made Joanna's chest prickle.

She did this five times before she exited the office, without taking anything. Joanna followed, almost running after her guide, as she let them down the corridor.

They, finally, entered the rest of the bar.

Atmospherically, it was butt ugly. From the walls decorated with miscellaneous crap to the giant swordfish strapped over the shelves of booze that stared menacingly at all who entered; to the bar stools that looked both unsteady and unpleasant to sit on; to the counters that were sticky from years of never-being-washed; to the brass bars that were cordoned underneath that had a bunch of dent marks in it, from men, and a couple of times women, getting their heads bashed in. If there ever were a place furthest from, and most forsaken by, God/s' beauty—it was *the Topspin*.

It smelled as bad as it looked. A fulsome dead-cat-stuffed-inside-a-forgotten-fish-tank smell that seemed to rise from the floorboards. It was unbearable.

"Yo fuck this," Zeno announced after a few moments of waving her illuminating phone around and finally noticing the deepening frown on Joanna's lips. "I thought maybe we could try instigating some alcoholic ghosts or something but this is just plain depressing. Worse than that, I'm bored. Let's bounce."

Joanna didn't argue.

They went out the same way they came in, back down the corridor and through the backdoor. Only as they descended the stairway, the smell that drove them out became stronger and fouler than before.

"Did you fart?" Joanna asked.

"No! Did you?"

"No."

"What the fuck…" Zeno whispered to herself, dumfounded. What kind of thing or combination of things could make such a stench?

Her question was answered with a growl. A low, primordial growl that made their guts clench and their hearts stop dead.

Panic grabbed Zeno by the throat and soon all she knew was terror.

Someone was in the room. Zeno knew it like she knew her name. Someone—something—was there—and they were standing next to her.

The muscles in her eyes twitched painfully as she strained to get them to move around the black stairwell because, despite all primal urges telling her not to look, she had to look. If she didn't, her heart would explode from fear of the unknown.

What she saw only decimated what little bravery she had. Standing at the bottom of the stairwell stood a demon. A white behemoth with the malformed body of an inbred horse standing on its hind legs. It had no skin and its body was riddled with black blood vessels and sinewy off-white muscles which rose and fell as It breathed laboriously. Black blood dripped out of its uncovered veins and onto the floor.

It stared back at them with the most hideous face she'd ever seen. Its snout dangled in front of its beady colorless eyes like the overgrown mouth of a deformed pig fetus. Its teeth bearing at her out of the lipless mouth. It had no nose, no lips, no hair, no skin. It stood there, breathing hard, like it was in pain, the air no doubt burning against its raw towering body.

It stood motionlessly as if waiting for the two women to run.

Zeno wanted so desperately to scream. To alert the whole world of the danger that laid ahead of them but her body froze, useless with fear. She couldn't flinch or jerk away from the creature who simply towered over them, so tall it had to bow its head to fit underneath the high ceiling.

The white horseman demon watched them, breathing hard, panting like it was starving.

Her lungs were aflame from the screams she couldn't release as she went petrified.

Then, the creature lowered its torso towards them, mouth opened like a freshly dug grave, and sank its giant, blood-soaked teeth around Joanna's head, squelching her screams with a single chomp.

Zeno ran while it chewed. She bolted back up the stairs for the drinking area. She was so quick she almost touched the front door. But before she could reach the door handle, the horse demon's shadow fell over her. Its long red teeth closing in around her skull.

5.

Zeno woke up with her hair wrapped around her face like a hijab, her face cased in drool, her body sopped in sweat.

She jerked upward, hoping to find Joanna beside her but found herself alone. She looked out the nearest window, hoping to find a comforting sun but found that the snowy world of yesterday had melted. Dead grass, mud rife with winter's litter, bare sickly trees, and a dull sky that offered no warmth or color awaited her. She sat there staring out the window until fragments of the nightmare clawed at her consciousness and she jumped out of bed to get away from the horrible room.

She found Fizzy eating the deathday cake Brynn had brought over on the living room couch.

"Morning," Fizzy greeted as she smacked her lips.

"Morning," Zeno returned, still bleary from sleep deprivation and silly fear. She glanced at the microwave's clock. It was eight am. She pawed at her aching head, wishing for sleep but her heart racing too fast for that to be an option. Oh, what she would have done for a cup of Turkish coffee.

"How you feeling?"

"Okay, I guess."

"Good." But her voice belied her statement.

"Why?" Zeno asked suspiciously.

Fizzy gave her a look of second-hand embarrassment. "Dude, you got *fucked* up last night."

"I did?"

"Dude. It was bad." She bit her lip then told her, "You got black-out drunk and asked Joanna to marry you."

Zeno groaned. *So, all of that was a dream*, she thought sadly. "No…! Don't say that." She flopped onto the couch cushion beside her and let out a loud, dejected moan. "Ugh! How did this happen?" Zeno made another despairing noise before she laid her head against Fizzy's shoulder. Fizzy used her free hand to rub her back, which Zeno appreciated in pitiful silence.

"Why are you up so early?" asked Fizzy.

"I got to print out an essay and hand it in then I got two midterms," Zeno replied with a yawn. "I wish it wasn't the last week before Spring Break. I slept like shit."

Fizzy offered her a spoonful of cake and said jokingly, "Fuck 'em. Stay home with me and watch me scream my head off while I apply for jobs all day."

She smiled as she bit into the spoon. "I wish." Then she pushed herself off the couch and said, as she headed towards the bathroom to take a shower and get herself ready for the day, "Maybe we'll luck out and inherit enough money from your grandma and we'll never have to work or school again."

Fizzy scoffed. "Yeah, right. The only thing I inherited from that was mental illnesses."

"That and your spiteful nature," Zeno added knowingly.

"Okay, that too," Fizzy said with a laugh.

6.

Fizzy had just opened her laptop to begin the process of finding a second job when her phone went off. She glanced at the screen and saw her other job's phone number pop up. She dismissed the call, assuming they were trying to call her in on her day off and proceeded to scroll through a job site.

Seconds after the call ended did her boss text her:

"An irate customer came in today saying you swore at him and told him to kill himself. This is unacceptable behavior. Your position with us has been terminated."

Fizzy stared at the text in utter disbelief. What person would come to her place of work just to lie like that? She was in such shock she immediately slammed her laptop shut and returned the missed call.

She tried to defend herself. "Whoever that was, they're either lying or mistaken! I would never tell a customer to kill themselves!" She insisted, though inwardly she thought, *to their face anyway.*

But her manager wouldn't hear it. "He was adamant that it was you. He knew you by name too. I'm sorry Odette but your position has been terminated."

Just like that, Fizzy was fired from her second job in less than a day. On her day off no less.

7.

With nowhere to go and no weed to smoke away the pain, she drove around, crying as she steered, parking her car on random roads until her tears left her restless and angry and she started her car up just because she could. She'd drive until the crying fit returned, parked her car when her tears were too thick to see and continued this pattern for hours.

She did this because she couldn't go home. Because going home meant having to tell Zeno and telling Zeno meant having to stand there and crush her own best friend's heart. Because if she didn't pay her half of the rent, they'd get kicked out of the apartment during the coldest time of the year.

Soon, her head was full of dark thoughts: Thoughts of their landlord gleefully stapling an eviction notice onto their door; thoughts of them shoving everything they owned into the single-car they shared; thoughts of cold nights in the backseat of a car overflowing with garbage; thoughts of them trying to squeeze themselves onto a single couch every night until the generosity of their friends and families runs out; thoughts of a women's shelter with not enough beds; thoughts of frostbite, hypothermia, starvation...

A thought of her frozen corpse laying in her backseat, stiff and blue with icicles hanging from her earlobes, produced the loudest sob. She already felt the fatigue, the ennui, the white-hot impulse for oblivion seep into her pores and wearing her down. She knew then and there if she didn't get some weed in her she would do something desperate and permeant.

She messaged every weed dealer she had saved in her phone and waited. But cruel fate, the weed dealers were dry! This sent her down another spiral of despair and she returned to her endless weeping, her forehead flat against her steering wheel, her red straw-like hair glued to her eyes from tears, saliva, and snot. She sat there, crying when the urge overwhelmed her then choking on air when her tear ducts gave up. She did this until the sun finished its time in the sky and the world dimmed slowly into a gradient of blues.

Eventually, the crying ceased and she was left puffy-eyed, empty-hearted, and exhausted. She looked out the window, hoping to indulge in a little people watching. But when her eyes turned to the streets all she saw found was more despair.

Without realizing it, she parked her car in the old business district which was nothing more than two rows of failed businesses standing side by side like chain-gangs comprised of dreams deferred. Her red-streaked eyes scanned the old signs and broken windows like she was respectfully reading the names off tombstones until her eyes struck something out of place.

There at the end of the block stood a business—a bar no less! —with a glowing open sign and electricity running.

She leaned underneath her windshield to read off the sign. *The Topspin.*

Fuck it, she thought, as she fished three dollars' worth of change from her cup holder, grabbed her identification card out of her glove compartment, and popped one leg into the road.

She sprinted down the sidewalk to escape the frigid world and didn't stop until she reached the entrance. When she pushed herself in, all the warmth that hid within rushed to claim her. She felt her stiff skin start to melt as she slid into an unused booth against the wall.

Almost six o'clock on a Thirsty Thursday and the bar was empty except for one patron who sat at the bar and another who sat in a booth by themself against the wall when you first walked in. She wondered why there were any patrons at all. A swordfish that stared menacingly at those upon entering. The barstools that looked both unsteady and unpleasant to sit on. The floors that were tessellated with the ugliest of colors the world had to offer (dried-blood-red, mustard yellow, baby barf green, and a brown that could only be described as a sick person's diarrhea).

It looks like Cheers *if it were designed by a colorblind hoarder*, she thought with a little bit of awe in the same way people are fascinated by the evolutionary patterns of wonky-eyed and snout-faced dogs.

And it smelled as bad as it looked. A faint feculent smell rose from the floorboards that she couldn't believe she didn't notice when she first walked in. She might have left if the thought of getting her coat back on, stepping back out into the cold, dark world, and going home to break her best friend's heart didn't sicken her more.

Within seconds, the terrible thoughts of yet to come came back. Moments later, she was slumped into herself, head against the sanitized table, and ready for another crying fit.

"You need a few minutes there?" A husky male voice asked her from above.

She looked up to see an impassive-looking bartender.

"Okay don't hate me but…" She began before dumping out the change from her pocket onto the table. "I'll take whatever…" She did a quick count. "Three bucks will get me."

"Hmm. Nothing off the food menu. But drink-wise you can either get a shot of the cheap stuff or a draft of the domesticated stuff."

"I'll take a shot of your cheapest tequila."

"Okay. Just let me see some ID." He said. When she gave him the card, he read it quickly. "Obiit." He glanced at her. "Is Darlene Sobriquet your mother?"

"Yes, she is." She said with pride. Despite everything going on, she loved her mother. And she loved it when people would ask her 'is Darlene your mother?'

"You knew her?"

"No, but I knew your grandmother."

"Oh."

"Yeah, she used to come to this bar all the time."

"Oh…that sucks for you."

"At least I wasn't related to her." He said as he gave her a tucked in grin then handed her back the card. "You want training wheels?" He asked, referring to salt and lime.

"Please."

"No problem, kid."

The man returned with the order to find Fizzy had stacked the change into small piles and kept them neatly on the edge of the table.

"Sorry again for the change." She said meekly as he placed the drink down in front of her. With a bashful chuckle, she added, "As you can tell, the struggle is real."

"Hey, money is money." He reassured as he shoveled the coins into his apron.

He watched her pick up the plastic shot glass and down the contents, her face contorted with disgust. He smiled. One of the few pleasures of the drinking industry was watching people's faces as they willingly drank poison.

When she opened her eyes, she found the bartender had put a second shot glass down in front of her. When she caught his eye, he looked away as if embarrassed.

"It's on the house."

She stared at the golden liquid with her face scrunched tight as she held back endeared tears. She raised the shot glass to him and whispered, "Thanks."

Affidious wordlessly returned to his post.

She downed the second drink, gagging the moment the spirit hit her throat but swallowed the poison whole. A gentle warmth flooded through her but did nothing to take away the sorrow devouring her soul. She used a sleeve to discreetly dry the new tears that followed, embarrassed by her public breakdown. She wondered how long this bartender would let her sit here with that one drink when a man's voice pulled her away from her thoughts.

"You're Jeanette's grandkid?" She looked up to see a man sitting on a stool with his head turned to her. He raised his glass to her and said, "My condolences to you and your family."

"Thanks," she said in a low voice.

He gave her a sympathetic smile. "Hey, I'm sure she's in a better place."

Fizzy stared at him for a second, confused by his odd choice of words, until it hit her. "Oh, you think…?" She snorted, unhinged by the liquor. She pointed at her tear-streaked face and affirmed, "Trust me these tears are *not* for Jeanette Sobriquet."

"Oh," he said, a little thrown off by her irreverence. "When I saw you coming into the bar crying, I thought—"

"Tits!" Affidious scolded.

"What! I meant no disrespect! I just thought that—"

"What did we say about thinking instead of drinking?" He muttered.

"It's okay," Fizzy interjected. "Really. I'm just crying over some other shit."

"Aww." Tits said, knowingly. "Boy trouble huh?"

"No?"

"Oh…girl trouble?"

"Tits!" Affidious hissed.

"What!" Tits cried. "I'm just trying to be inclusive."

"I doubt she wants to talk about her problems with a Nosy Parks like you." Affidious snapped.

"Not really." Fizzy confessed in a small cracking voice. As her cheeks started to turn red, she said, "Unless you guys happen to know who's willing to hire a fuck up who just lost two jobs in one day."

115

Affidious and Tits watched as Fizzy crumpled over the table and began to cry.

"You lost two jobs?" Affidious asked. "The day after your grandmother died?"

"Uh-huh," Fizzy said, her head pressed against the glass top, her back convulsing as she succumbed, yet again, to tears. But she squelched the tears quickly and lifted her head to the two men, adding, "But I got the last laugh though. I called OSHA and the Department of Labor on both those places. They're about to lose half their overnight crew AND get a buttload of fines."

"Aye, that's the spirit." Tits cheered. "Hey, you know what? It's their loss. I bet you were a heck of a worker. And I bet you'll find a new job in no time."

Fizzy didn't believe either of those things. She knew she wasn't going to find a job quickly for the simple reason that she had spent the better part of the last two years trying to find a good enough to job to replace the two crummy ones she currently had. The idea of finding one job that would pay somewhat decently felt like a pipedream. But she didn't have the time nor energy to explain all that to the well-meaning stranger. Instead, she nodded her head at him, bent her head down, and resumed quietly bawling her eyes out.

In those breaths where Fizzy's will to live incinerated underneath a cheapo chandelier, something within Affidious bloomed. Thanks to his long career in bartending, he would come to know a multitude of sob cases over the years—people who, for whatever reason, were simply magnets to all of life's misfortunes—but Fizzy had to be one of the most pitiful people he'd ever laid his eyes upon. Being Jeanette Sobriquet's grandkid alone would have made him feel sorry for her but to be all of that and broke? It was enough to break any bastard's heart. Including his.

He glanced over at Tits, who as if reading his mind, nodded and Affidious took his apron off, quietly setting it on the space beside his regular so the coins wouldn't jangle too loudly, and walked over to Fizzy's table.

He made his presence known with a cough before taking the seat opposite her. She lifted her head but didn't bother wiping at her tear-stained face.

"Listen, um, one of my dishwashers quit and I could use someone for the lunch rush tomorrow..."

"You-you're offering me a job?" Fizzy asked as she used the back of her hand to rub around her eyes. "Even after I said all that stuff about calling OSHA on my job and swiping office supplies?"

"Hey what do I care—wait, you didn't say anything about stealing from the place."

"Oh. That's because I would never." She said quickly.

Affidious smiled. *Petty, spiteful, and a practiced liar. She's definitely Jeanette's kin.* "Twenty bucks an hour. You can start tomorrow. How's that sound?"

She went so quiet for a fearful moment he thought she was going to haggle the pay scale on him. But instead, she got up, took two baby steps around the table, and threw her arms around him.

"Thank you," she whispered, her voice already breaking from the onslaught of new tears. "Thank you so much." When she let go of him, she said, "You have no idea how much I appreciate this. I promise you won't regret this."

"I know I won't kid." He said. "Does nine am work for you?"

"Whatever works for you, works for me."

"Good shit. I'll see you then."

Fizzy shook his hand, grabbed her coat, thanked him half-dozen times more before she skipped out of the bar, and back into the cold. It wasn't until she reached the car that she realized she never asked his name.

"You're a much better man than I am, Fiddy." Tits said once she was gone. "I wouldn't have done shit for the kid. I would've just taken her money, told her and her shitty bloodline to kick rocks, and to not let the door hit your ass on the way out."

Affidious shrugged, ignoring the Wraith's impenetrable stares that pierced him from across the room as he said, "What can I say? I'm a nice guy."

Fizzy accumulated twenty missed calls from her mother by the time she returned to 1215 Carter Street and another, staggering, forty-seven texts from her siblings all demanding she call their mother back.

"You can't ignore your family forever," Zeno warned.

"I'm not," she insisted as she turned her phone off for the rest of the night. "I'm just going to ignore them until after the funeral."

8.

Friday

Tomorrow couldn't come fast enough. Though Fizzy despised having to work a third of her life away for shit pay, nothing could beat the first day thrills. The thrill of starting something new, the gratefulness of staving off poverty, the joy of knowing nobody expected anything out of her (for a day or so). It was a feeling she'd been chasing since she entered the working-class realm. It was a feeling that never got tiresome. That first day, that sweet newness.

On that fateful Friday, Fizzy woke up to the sound of her downstairs neighbor having one of his early morning mental breakdowns. It was seven am.

The screams came in bursts but were consistent bursts of nonsense words (Radda ba ma fadda), curses (shit-muffin), damnations (it's a metaphor you whore!), and finally plain old accusations (you're Satan's shoelace!).

Fizzy listened to all of it with a groggy disinterest. They became as ritualistic as bird calls in the morning, to the point where on days where she went against routine, she could sleep through them. Sometimes, on those cruel days when the body woke up on its own without the need for an alarm clock, she would lay in bed for a minute or two, checking her phone, while she waited for the screams to shoot her out of the covers.

The screams belonged to Grandpa Claus, her downstairs neighbor's father who moved into the duplex a few years ago and never left.

She woke up to Grandpa Claus's outbursts with magnanimity. When she climbed out of bed and traipsed to the bathroom sink to begin her skincare regiment and overheard the older man scream out "don't piss in my ear and call it lemonade!" she quietly laughed and said, "Mood."

On her better days, when she got a glorious night's sleep and wasn't burning with white-hot anxiety, she empathically tuned out the old man's screams the way adults, who raised small children or are sympathetic to the moodiness of small children, quietly ignored a toddler's meltdown in a public space.

More than a few times though, on those terrible mornings where she can't be bothered to sympathize with herself let alone others, she'd scream right back. She'd lay in her bed, frustrated to near-insanity from lack of sleep and fraught with ennui, and bellow at the stucco ceiling until her whole body trembled. Sometimes, she'd leap to the ground, touch her nose to the ground, and scream at the man downstairs to shut the fuck up. But, as if they competed with each other to see who had the worse mental illness, Grandpa Claus would howl longer and harder than she ever could (with copious amounts of "go away Satan!" thrown in which never failed to make her hate herself later) and she would slink back into her pink comforter all sobs and shame and defeat.

Those days were far and few and infrequent as with time comes adaptabilities. In the last few years, she stocked up on earplugs, she kept to a regular bedtime that went around Grandpa Claus's (thank god she lived with Early Bird Zeno who loved any excuse to be boring and go to bed before eight o'clock). She even took up smoking weed before bed which she noticed gave her the luxuriance of a drunkard's sleep without feeling like shit the next day.

By eight forty-five am she emerged from her home, self-loathing at a concealable low, and ventured down the front porch steps, past the old brown man with an enormous belly in three bright red hoodies and a thick white beard emitting thick shaggy clouds from his corncob pipe.

"' Morning," she greeted, not expecting a return.

Grandpa Claus didn't hear her through the giant headphones he wore and even then, his rheumy eyes were fixed on the road ahead.

She jammed her key into her car door and climbed in. "Bye Mr. Petito," she cried before slamming the door shut. Her head was bent over her phone as she thumbed through her musical options. At that time, she missed Grandpa Claus pull his corncob pipe from between his chapped, wonder loudly, "Blue-yellow Lone Ranger (incoherent) balls for ketchup packets and loosies."

Translation: "That car with the Bosnian flag has been sitting in front of our house all day and night since yesterday. I wonder if they're living in their car."

But Fizzy didn't speak word salad. Even if she did, she didn't catch a word of what he said for she was already pulling out of the driveway.

9.

Before Fizzy did anything involving work, she went to the corner store. Five to seven times a week, sometimes more, she could be found buying some form of an energy drink at the bodega around the corner. Energy drinks: for some, they're liquid heart attack to others they're slurp-able life force and she was the self-aware group who knew they were the former but got addicted to them because how else are you supposed to work a third of your life away? Every day, she pulled her rusted-to-shit car and coasted over man-sized potholes that took up sixty percent of the parking lot, risking popping a tire or wearing down her brakes, and wrecking her ball bearings, because she couldn't imagine starting her day, without sugary caffeine to help her through the drudgery.

She parked directly in front of the red, white, and blue brick-laden store. In a spot next to the entrance sat a Black man perched on top of a milk crate, his torso bent over himself as if in pain or fallen asleep or both. His milk crate was underneath a barred-up window where overlapping images of tobacco, beer, ice cream, and beautiful women jumped out at you.

When she walked to the front door, the man on the milk crate uncurled himself, like he was made of flower petals, and looked right at her. For a moment, she feared he was going to catcall her.

"' Morning miss."

"Good morning."

"I'd hate to bother you but do you have a cigarette?"

"I don't smoke. Sorry."

"That's okay," he said as she side-stepped over the ringing threshold. Before the door closed her into the incense and wet-newspaper smelling store, she heard him say, "You have a blessed day, miss."

She pivoted for the florescent light cooler that held all the sugary drinks and retrieved a twelve ouncer of Zeus Juice, a black and gold aluminum can. Half the can was webbed with gold lightning while the section where its'

125

product name sat on a neon purple cloud. The label on the back told you that juice was criminally misleading, if anything it was a carbonated kidney failure waiting to happen, but when did blatant false advertisement ever stop anything. It didn't stop her from stepping into line with it.

As she waited for a middle-aged woman to decide which lottery ticket to funnel all her hopes and dreams into, the door opened and rang again. Fizzy heard, without looking, an older man step into line and grumble something about "bums" underneath his breath.

His voice trailed off, where she hoped his opinion would follow into silence. But it was a (white) man's opinion so of course, it could not die without being heard first.

"Hey, Habibi!" The man behind her called out to the cashier. "You got a guy in front of your store trying to bum off of people."

Fizzy knew the cashier knew of the man outside, given there usually was one or two out there whenever she was there, but of course he had to show his customer his voice was heard. The cashier looked up and peered around the rack of gummy candies as if to catch a glance of this panhandler. "Oh, oh-oh," the cashier let out, apologetically, as if this is somehow his fault, "I see. I'm very busy now but I'll take care of 'em when the line is done."

"See that you do." The man said. "Nobody wants to be harassed like that first thing in the morning."

His emphasis on the word harassed made her nose twitch.

"Yes, yes, yes, I agree," the cashier said quickly as he rang out the next person's order than darted their eyes towards Fizzy.

She put her drink on the armpit tall counter and dug into her clutch for her money.

"Anything else?"

"Yeah. A lighter and a pack of *Newports*, please."

When she got outside the man on the milk crate had scooted himself to the farthest edge of the concrete ledge. She walked up to him and handed him the cigarettes and the lighter with one hand. He received them both with his hands pressed together like he was collecting rainwater.

"I hope this is your brand," she told him meekly, afraid now he didn't like menthol.

He thanked her with direct eye contact and she suddenly felt so spoiled and presumptuously. What if he only wanted a cigarette because he was trying to squelch

127

his hunger? She should've just given him the eleven dollars. But she never carried cash and the ATM inside would've taken too long. By then the man inside would've gotten his wish and the cashier would've shooed him away like an incorrigible stray.

She told him to have a good day, making sure to add sir, although she feared, later, that was an error too (who was she to assume?) and she walked away depressed at the world for being so depressing. She almost ruined her makeup when she got back into her car but she held back errant tears and made her way to *the Topspin*.

10.

The jitters came the moment she stepped out of the car and went to the entrance. When she reached for the doorknob, she was dismayed to find it locked. What if he doesn't remember giving her the job? What if it was a mean joke? What if he turns out to be a creep who follows her from room to room with evil intent? Or worse, what if the job sucks? What will she do then?

You'll keep it until you find a new one, a stern part of herself instructed but that only made her guts crinkle and steam.

You never know, said another hopeful voice as she knocked on the door and waited. *That bartender seemed nice. Maybe you'll like this job.*

She didn't wait long before she heard the sounds of his heavy feet approach the front door. She could see the

Black man with the orange hair gander at her through the collage of beer advertisements blocking the door window.

"You're right on time," he remarked when he opened the door for her. He stepped aside to let her in. The first thing she noticed when she entered the unlit bar was the smell from yesterday had dissipated. *Must have been garbage night*, she thought.

"You know yesterday I got so excited," said Fizzy as she followed him through the bar. "I never asked you your name."

He stopped walking and offered his large hand. "Affidious Dixon. But call me Fiddy if you like."

"Okay. But only if you call me Fizzy." She said as they shook hands.

"Deal." He said with a smile. "I got work shirts downstairs," he explained as she followed him down a small hallway together not far from the bar area. "What size are you?"

"Med—"

"Shit, I forgot something." He said abruptly, turning around and heading through a door that led into a shadowy stairwell. He turned his head over his shoulder and told her, "Make yourself comfortable at the bar. I got to grab something."

Taking the advice, she took a seat on a stool and watched him disappear into the basement.

11.

Zeno was on the city bus, making her way home after a long, arduous morning of test-taking. She was half-asleep, head felled backward, slowly drifting towards the snoring land when the bus driver slammed on the brakes and she was jerked out of her reverie.

When her eyes opened, she watched a middle-aged white man head towards the back of the bus where she sat.

Oh fuck, don't sit next to me don't sit next to me don't sit next to me...

Of course, out of all the seats available to him, this man had to choose the one next to her. Worse, he even smiled at her, making it clear he wanted to engage in conversation with her.

"Dobra jutro," he said kindly.

She returned the greeting, her voice lowering unintentionally out of respect, the way it always did when she spoke to older Bosnians.

He smiled at her, as if happy to have someone to talk to finally. She groaned inwardly, fearing this stranger would confuse her forced kindness as a sign that she was someone he could dump all her problems onto. Or, worse, that it was a sign of her love for him.

"How are you?" He asked as if they were old friends.

"I'm fine." She replied in her first language. "And you?"

"Good." Then he leaned forward slightly and asked, "Where's your family from?"

"Banja Luka."

"Banja Luka." He said it in a breathy quality as his eyes shone over wistfully. "I used to have a house out there."

"Really?" She said, feigning interest.

"Yes. Maybe our families knew each other. Who are your parents?"

"My mom's Tonya Begic, my father was Armin Zenovenovic."

He thought over the names then smiled. "I remember your parents…" His smile faltered, slightly, when he added, "It must have been hard on your mother with your father's passing."

She frowned slightly. *No shit*, she wanted to say but instead, she said, "It was."

He offered condolences, then the adage, which she heard a thousand times throughout her life whenever her dead father was brought up, "Pokju Armin." (Peace to Armin's soul)

She thanked him quietly, glancing out the window, hoping he'll notice her disinterest in this conversation.

He did not, or if he did, he chose to ignore it, for he continued, "How is your mother by the way? From what I remember…she was very pretty."

Zeno didn't say anything for an uneasy feeling began to grow in her stomach. Something in her guts told her to get away from this man. To get up and put as much distance as she could between herself and this man. But she was miles from her stop. And the only other person on the bus was the driver who, at that moment, felt as far away as China.

He gave her a wolfish smile and said, in a mixture of Bosnian and Serbian, "You look just like her."

When his voice changed, fresh terror reared up within her as the interior of the bus vanished. Along with the ice and the snow and the paved city streets. Suddenly she was on a pebbly road and the smell of fire and gun smoke pierced her nose. She was being carried by her mother who sobbed as she ran with her. Zeno remembered watching a soldier shoot a man in the back of the head and watching the man's skull crack open when his head hit the road like a watermelon. When she looked over her mother's shoulder, she caught the rebel leader's eyes and how they were the prettiest kind of blue. It wasn't until she got older that she found out the man, whose murder formulated her earliest memory, was her father.

"Do you remember me, child?" He asked her but she was so far away at that moment his voice sounded like it came from the bottom of a lake.

Her eyes were wide, panicked, like a startled deer's. She realized she knew his face.

He smiled at her wild fear.

"Please don't hurt me," she begged quietly, as she sunk deeper into her chair.

"Oh, trust me, child. If I wanted to, I would've already." The Wraith said, his voice so gentle one would've thought he said it out of kindness. He slapped his knees as if getting ready to stand and said, "No, I have no interest in hurting you."

"I don't have any—"

"I don't want anything from *you*." He cut in sharply, in a voice that said, *don't interrupt me again.* "No, what I want is for you to convince your friend to stop being so damn stubborn."

"I don't…"

"Your friend, uh," He snapped his fingers trying to jog his memory. "Pepsi?"

"F-Fizzy?"

"Yes, Fizzy." He said it two more times, enjoying the way it sounded. "Fizzy, Fizzy." Then in a sing-song voice, "Stubborn Fizzy." He tucked his tongue. "Disrespectful child that one is." He wagged his finger at her and chided her gently like she was a naughty child caught with their hand in the cookie jar, "How can you let your friend go around speaking ill of her dead grandmother like that?"

She sat speechlessly, stuck somewhere between the surrealness of being scolded by a war criminal about respecting the dead and being steeled by the terror of knowing she was trapped in a conversation with pure evil.

"Dishonoring the dead is one thing but to dishonor your dead family?" He shook his head. "If I were her father," He flung his arm down like he was whipping the ground, "I'd beat her like a dog."

"What do you want?" She demanded in a small shaky voice.

He gave her an odd smile, then he poked her on the knee, once, his very touch made her body wither and squirm, and said, "Tell your friend to go to her grandmother's funeral."

Zeno's eyebrows jumped to her hairline. Was this deranged man being serious? "Why?"

He never answered. He simply gave her another peculiar smile as he reached above him and yanked on the cord. In the short time it took the bus to slow to a stop, he didn't say a word. He merely kept smiling at her, like she was a precocious child he caught trying to steal cookies from an unmanned cookie jar while she tried to bury herself within her seat.

Eventually, the bus came to a stop and he stood up with a spring in his step, telling her, with a pointed look in his eyes, "Vidimose."

She watched him leave the bus, her heart beating so hard it felt like someone was performing CPR on the inside of her chest, but when she looked out the window, to see if his horrible blues eyes still followed her, the Wraith had vanished.

12.

Fizzy was surreptitiously texting Zeno about her morning went when a loud bang made her jump.

What the actual fuck... She thought as her ears strained to make sense of what she just heard.

CLOMP! CLOMP!

She jumped, her phone nearly flying out of her loose hands, as the third clomping sound rang throughout the bar.

She twisted her neck around, searching for the source.

Her chest seized and burned as the air around her turned sharp and thin. *Someone's in the bar*, she knew. Her ears darted around in the dim-light in search of a knife but found none. Not even a small one used for lemons and limes. The closest thing to her were those little white mugs and she grabbed one and held it in her left hand like a softball as she pinned herself against the wall.

CLOMP! CLOMP!

They were huge, she concluded from the way they created thunder in the floorboards. She imagined a man twice her weight and size, choosing to walk slowly, putting a small metal plate on his shoes just to fuck with her, deliberately trying to terrorize her with his slow, heavy steps. Savoring the terror that threatened to grip her like a heart attack as he—they—whoever—made their way into the room she stood in, preparing themselves for whatever horrible, violent act they were going to commit.

She sucked back a small gasp as petrified tears ran down her cheeks. *This was it*, she thought as she swallowed down a sob that would've drew the predator in faster. She was almost spared. She was almost lucky.

She dug her right hand into her coat pocket and held her car key in her hand like a knife.

They are closer, she realized the sound pinging off of her ears like it was against the floor. She pressed herself further into the open space between the wall of liquor and the regular wall, that—thank fuck—her rectangular-shaped ass was somehow able to squeeze into without knocking anything over.

CLOMP! CLOMP!

Blood pumped through her head like she was standing next to a waterfall and brought on a fierce headache that she feared would've caused her to pass out.

No more footsteps came for what felt like eons. She waited. And listened for movement but heard none.

She expected him—them—to look for her throughout the room. Even call for her, like a sick villain. But full minutes went by with nothing. The muscles in her arm started to ache from holding the mug from the waiting. The whole time she stood in the corner, her eyes were kept on the door which stood mere paces away. If she could get past the counter…

But she clenched her entire body with fear at the thought of running. She wasn't fast and graceful like Zeno who she imagined could leap over the counter and sail out of the room in mere seconds while she, stagnant Fizzy, favorite-thing-to-do-is-nothing Fizzy, hadn't jogged—let alone run—since the middle school when they finally gave up on trying to kill fat kids and banned the Presidential Fitness test.

She thought of her mother in all black, sobbing hysterically in front of her rented coffin, while tear-soaked Zeno tried to hold her up but she's so overwhelmed by devasting grief she can't be held upright, she's simply dangling by the elbows. She imagined her siblings and friends howling at her wooden box in unending pain. She imagined herself, a restless ghost, standing beside the coffin, weeping quietly into the void because she could not do anything to stop this anguish.

So often she feared loved ones' deaths and what would happen to her after that unthinkable day, she mentally begged Death to bury her first. But standing there, trapped between a cash register and a sticky wall of booze, waiting for her rapist and or murderer to find her, she pleaded with Death, for the first time in her life, to leave her alone.

She slowly let go of her car key and carefully pulled her hand out of her pocket as she raised it to the ledge where the coffee pot sat, unaware of her danger. She reached down until her fingers brushed against the glass. Her fingertips burned at once. Slowly, she poked the white handle until it faced her entirely. Then, with a shaking arm, she grabbed the handle and began to lift it from the hot plate. Her arm shook furiously but she tried to keep the coffee pot steady even though this was her less dominated hand. She had it halfway off when a driblet of coffee sprung from the pot and sizzled to its death.

She could hear movement again, this time it came towards her—this time it wasn't walking it was running—and with nothing else, she pulled herself out of the corner, yanked the coffeepot from its maker, spun around, and heaved several ounces of piping hot black liquid directly into the predator's face.

An agonizing bray of a horse being branded erupted from the creature she attacked, which she saw in a few breaths of perplexed terror when she found herself unable to run was far from human.

What jerked and flayed violently before she was a lumbering creature, exceeding seven feet tall, with skin the color of expired milk and the texture of something burnt but also raw. It flayed backward on crooked legs and she watched in bewilderment as it trampled backward on the floorboards in cracked hooves, two of its scraggly, clawed arms reaching for its face while a third, ingrown-looking one hung from its chest useless.

As it writhed in pain, she scurried from behind the bar and charged the door, her stringy legs pumping harder than they've ever pumped before. The creature's screams split her ears and, in her mind, it was already behind her, chasing her. She yanked the doorknob open, the door banging behind her like a shotgun going off and she ran.

143

She didn't stop when the whiteness of the world blind her within seconds. Snow pelted the world around her and she staggered as it stabbed her eyes, the whiteness and the water burned her unadjusted pupils. By the time her eyes could open fully, she could see her car. It stood in the snowy street like adorably ugly stead. She was on the road then she was next to the car. Her heart ricocheted off her chest like a cascade of bullets as she slid her car keys into the door. She threw herself into the car and slammed the door behind her, locking it as soon as her ass hit the seat. She sat there for a second, panting wildly as her jangling hand tried to bring her keys to the ignition.

When the car roared to life, she let out an exhilarate cry. Her sense of safety returned, slowly but beautifully, as she cinched the seat belt in.

She was about to yank the car into drive, her hand halfway towards the power stick when the car spun on its side and slapped her, like a bug, into oblivion.

13.

Fizzy woke up, hanging sideways, floating like a fly caught on a single thread of web. She tried to lift her head but was rewarded with searing pain that ran through her neck and shot into the back of her skull like she was injected with glass. When she opened her mouth to cry, a pool of blood that she wasn't aware she was swallowing rained out of her and splattered diagonally. For a few agonizing breaths, she didn't know anything except blood and pain.

When she opened her eyes again, she saw that she was hanging above a car door, the seat belt cutting into her abdomen like a botched operation. Little, light blue shards of broken window glass sprayed the bottom of her like pixelated water. She gasped when looked down at herself and found that she was half sitting, half hanging. Her car had been thrown off its wheels.

She struggled to unbuckle the flat gray garrote, her fingers hovered, frantically, just out of reach of the red release button. The seat belt dug deeper and deeper into her stomach, blood sluiced out of her like a slashed juice box. White-hot pain flooded her insides until she could barely hear her own screams. Little white clouds crept into the corners of her eyes, threatening to snuff her vision out under a blanket of oblivion. Soon, warm blood saturated her legs and her feet and dripped into the rest of the car. She felt her body start to sag and for a moment she felt death slowly wash over her and after so much pain, she was too tired to be afraid.

But then gravity snapped. Her seat belt broke apart under the weight of her. And Fizzy hurtled into swift, comforting, darkness.

A vile, rotten meat smell dragged her by the nose back into consciousness. She opened her eyes but found the act far too painful as blinding white made her eyelids snap shut. She could smell blood and gasoline. She felt broken glass digging into her face but when she tried to lift her head she was rewarded with searing pain. Terror razored through her and she made a small pip of a cry.

Then came the crunchy sound of someone walking on glass.

She saw a pair of men's shoes come towards her but she was couldn't move. So, she squeezed her eyes shut and willed herself to fall back into unconsciousness. She passed out to the screeching sounds of metal being dragged across the concrete, too hurt to care that she was dying.

She was floating in and out of consciousness when she heard a man's voice from above say, "Either go to Jeanette's funeral…" She opened her eyes but it was too painful for her to see who was talking to her. All she could make out was the outline of two men—one black and one white—carrying her. The last thing she heard before she slipped back into the voice was one of the men telling her, "Or attend your own."

14.

Fizzy woke up to the sound of animals screaming.

She lifted her head only to find that it weighed much more than her neck could support. She reached for her skull only to find that her hands were gone.

This was bad.

Pain and dread exploded through her like a grenade as she struggled to explain the inexplicable to herself.

Where am I? She thought. *How did I get hurt? Did someone hurt me? Did I hurt me?*

She had no answers for any of it.

The only thing she knew for certain was that she fucked up somehow. In some exponential, irreparable, ruinous way. How? She couldn't remember.

She was laying on something. Hard. Was this her bed? No. She knew, with vague certainty, that beds weren't supposed to be this hard. Her cheek was squished against something hard but cool. Concrete? The word sprang out of the darkness. It felt like a foreign word that she should've known but didn't quite remember. When she moved her face from side to side little rocks, only slightly bigger than sand, rolled in the direction she took them in.

Her forehead was pressed against something sharp but every time she tried to turn her head, a lightning bolt of pain greeted her. She made a sharp inhale of pain and accidentally swallowed some rocks, which hit the back of her throat and choked her. She coughed, painfully, and was punished with more pain. "Why is this happening?" She screamed inwardly.

"You're going to die here," a voice in her head told her.

"Shut up," another voice spoke up for her and though she was grateful that it stood up to that pushy little creep, she also knew that the first voice was right. She had to get out of this hole, somehow. Emphasis on how.

Time passed fear grew. She tried screaming for help, hoping against all hope to get someone's attention but this only served to weaken her voice and accidentally swallow more pebbles.

She leaned to her left then to her right then back to the left. The plan, which hung in the peripheries of her consciousness, was to roll onto her back. She thought herself like that creature, who she could see so easily in her mind, with the shell on its back.

"You mean a turtle?" A snarky voice reminded her.

"Yes! A turtle!" The remembrance of the word made her insides flutter hopefully. If she could just turtle her way out of this…

Turtles who roll onto their back die, genius.

"SHUT UP!"

She leaned onto her hip bone, until one buttcheek was in the air, then let it drop.

Her forehead was gushing with sweat. A torrent of swears and strained grunts poured out of her as her body rocked from side to side until the fiery pain proved too much and she rolled flat against the ground, panting in defeat.

"Use your hands, dumbass." A voice that sounded like her mother told her.

"I can't. I don't have any."

"Yes, you do! Push!"

She clenched her teeth, ready to berate the phantom's voice when she felt something behind her—

muscles shaking, quaking, resisting. She felt the pebbles and dirt beneath her shake and watched, baffled, as her forehead lifted from the ground, her torso raised until, finally, she was sitting upward.

She gasped, overjoyed but when she looked down for her hands they were still gone. So were her boobs. She dipped her head down, despite the pain, to inspect and found that she was staring, directly, at her ass.

"What the—" She bent her head, gingerly, making sure she was seeing things correctly. She was staring at her own back. "How—" She tried to turn her head but found that impossible. Pain shot into her skull and left her panting, sweating, crying.

"What was happening?" She asked herself impotently.

She looked ahead and discovered at last that she was sitting in a hole in the middle of an empty street. Or, what she assumed was a road. It was hard to tell.

The sky and the ground muddled together in a swatch of reddish-gray. What she called a street laid out before her, endlessly wide and straight. She had to use her hands to prop herself up, turn her slightly, put herself down, then pick herself back up just to see what was going on.

Nothing.

Absolutely nothing.

There was a total absence of noise, like a graveyard in the dead of winter. Only less so for there wasn't any traffic noise in the distance or birds or squirrels, yapping dogs, people. No nature of any kind. Worse, there were no smells. No gas exhaust, no garbage, no nicotine smoke, no regular smoke, no dirt or mud or trees, or the smells of food. There was a total lack of human life and that absence pierced her soul.

"I'm dead," she concluded finally. "I'm dead. I died.

"But how did you die?" A second voice asked, fretfully.

"Who cares?" But that didn't stifle the little nagging voice in her soul that needed reassurance. "I have to be dead," she told herself.

Then, at once, a thunderous clap erupted out of the sky. The suddenness made her snap her neck, involuntarily, sending tremendous pain down her spine. She sobbed, hurt, and scared. She instinctively tried to hold herself but her arms flailed helplessly behind her.

Then it donned on her. She looked at her shoulders out of the corner of her eye. To her horror, she saw only the smooth back of her shoulder. She sent a conscious message to herself to reach backward and after great effort, her body complied and she saw the tips of her fingers waving back at her.

So that's how I died. She thought wryly. *I snapped my neck.* The idea appalled her. She saw herself tripping down the stairs at home, her head bent down to her phone as she compiled a text, not paying attention, her feet missing a crucial step, and her body crashing into the ground, her skull severed from the brain stem, her neck snapped backward.

A smile tugged on the corners of her lips. It's not how she would've wanted to go, but it was a fitting end nonetheless. The anxieties that jumbled her nerves before slipped away from her.

She looked around, her eyeballs pushing violently as she tried to seek out the world around her. But it was horribly limiting and, after the umpteenth time of trying to turn her neck just to get stabbed in the face with pain, she said, "fuck it". Reaching up and over, she put one hand underneath the pit of her neck and one at the base of her crown. Then, she counted to three and in one swift moment, yanked her head back into place.

The pain was unbearable. It made her knees buckle and hot tears rolled down her cheeks as she wept from the agony. It took some time but the searing pain eventually died into a pulsating numbness. At some point, it died altogether. She tested it out, swiveling her head left to right freely. When she looked right, that is when she discovered that she was not alone.

A stone's throw away, she spotted two bodies, one body had its hand pressed into the trunk while the other was hunched over, humping furiously. They both had erections, they both wore layers upon layers of faded clothes, and both of them, to her horror and fascination, did not have heads.

She watched the two of them go on like this, their bodies colliding into each other at a fantastic speed, fleshing against flesh producing the clapping noise that spooked her earlier.

"Stop staring," her grandmother's voice scolded. "Give them some privacy for fuck's sake."

She looked away, sending her sight back on her body which she then realized was still sitting on the hole.

"It's a called pothole," another voice told her. "And you hate potholes."

"Ew, you're right."

154

She got up, surprised to find that her legs worked fine, though they were a little wobbly.

She looked over her shoulder again at the two bodies, who continued without shame. Beyond them lay a vast expansion of muted redness. She turned her head, expecting the opposite direction to offer the same, as it did moments earlier.

Off in the distance, stood the demon. That towering, hideous horse-man demon, staring back at her. Though she was too far to see its eyes, she knew they were focused on her and her only. From there, she could hear its husky breath. Parched for her blood.

She u-turned violently and ran, her feet slapping against the gray ground, bolting past the two headless lovers. She ran despite the seizure in her heart, the constriction in her throat, the dizzying spell that settled over her eyes.

She ran for what felt like hours.

15.

Fizzy knew she fucked up when she woke up in a
pothole. She felt the pebbles pinch the side of her face
before she felt the scorching sunburn on her back. She was
already ashamed and didn't know what for. Just like
yesterday and the day before.

16.

She woke up every day, baked and bloody, only to spend it running. It's all she did. She ran when she got up, hid when she couldn't run, and when she couldn't stop herself, she'd look behind her. But no matter how long she ran and hid, no matter how long she went without looking, there it was. In the distance. Standing, watching her.

It went like this: She'd run. It'd follow. She'd hide. It would find her. She'd crash into an exhausted heap, wake up and repeat.

One day she was running and she ran out of land.

She didn't realize so until the last second when she almost ran herself off the edge. She stopped in time for her toes to skid right over the ledge.

Before her, laid a burning sea of white. She tried to look down, to gauge it, but the longer she stood there the worst the white burned.

Eventually, she had to turn her head, eyes burning. She held her palms to her eyes until the darkness and the navy stars soothed her aching pupils. When she could see again, she discovered it towered over her.

She fell backward, hoping she'd land in oblivion, only to land on her spine.

It peered at her. Its hideous face boring into her, murderously.

She held her arms above her face and braced for the inevitable blows when a voice she hadn't heard in years bespoke, "Odette?"

Fizzy opened her eyes. The creature had backed away a touch. It stopped at the end of her shadow, as if out of respect.

"N-no."

"You're lying."

"N—" She stopped herself. "I mean, yes. Sorry. I lie when I'm scared."

"You're scared of me?" She blinked. Was she imaging or did it sound…hurt? She lowered her hands, slowly, to look at it better.

She watched it watch her. What was it waiting for? Was it taking a break from chasing her, letting her slip into a false sense of security? Would it snap her neck if she tried to move too fast? Or was it something else?

"Should I be scared of you?" She asked finally.

"I would hope not." It replied without moving its mouth. But the strangest part was it sounded sad like she had dashed its hopes somehow. "We are the same."

"You're...human?"

"No. I meant we're both living beings."

"I'm—I'm alive?" She asked, shocked.

"Yes."

She turned her head to its side. In the distance, she saw the simmering dots of people. She pointed with her nose. "Are they?"

"I have no idea."

She turned her head back at him. "Is this...?" She trailed off, hoping it would know what she meant. Fortunately, it did.

"No."

"Oh." She breathed a little easier. But then the questions kept tumbling in and panic started to fold in on her. "Okay so if I'm not dead and this isn't the afterlife...then where are we?"

"We're in the land of wherever dreams take place."

"…Really?"

It nodded as if it were obvious.

She tossed her head to the side to take another lasting look at the red land of carnage, the headless homeless people, the exploding suns. "Damn…" She muttered. "I really should go to therapy."

They did this little staring contest until Fizzy's back ached from the hard ground. She slid her shoulders back until her hands were next to her hips and propped herself into a seated position. It allowed her to do so, patiently.

She pulled her knees to her chest and they resumed their little game. Until, it, sounding so desolate, asked, "You don't remember me, do you?"

She shook her head. "Sorry." It wilted when she said that and a piece of her heart broke off. But her mind caught up with the rest of her and she added, "But your voice sounds familiar."

It must have sensed her honesty because it perked immediately when she said this.

"That makes me so happy," It said, pulling its mouth back until all four rows of teeth were curved at her. She flinched under its smile. Noticing her discomfort, it neutralized its face and asked, "Would it help if I told you my name?"

She scoffed. "Good luck. I mean, go for it. But I'm gonna be honest with you. Trauma and years of being a heavy weed smoking took away most of my memories."

It crouched on its hind legs until its bony knee caps were directly at her eye level, stuck one hoof out, and introduced itself, "My name is PJ Clements. And you and I used to be very good friends."

19.

A lot of children had or have an imaginary friend or two growing up. Some base them off things they've seen on TV or children they would like to be friends with. Some befriend the lonely ghosts that live in their dwellings. Then there's prepubescent Fizzy, whose imaginary friend was a seven-foot-tall spider-horse-man demon that she befriended shortly after Darlene's second stint in rehab and was forced to live with Grandma Sobriquet.

"PJ!" Her hippocampus crackled to life with memories she hadn't realized she'd forgotten. She sprung up to embrace her but when her hand touched its body, she felt the rawhide latch onto her. She watched as vine-like blood vessels coiled around her hand as if trying to eat her. She screamed, yanked her arm until, with its help, she broke free. She looked at her hand and found redness.

"What the actual fuck was that?" She demanded.

"That wasn't me." PJ insisted. "It's my body. Ever since I lost my skin, it's been insatiable."

"Awww…PJ. What happened to your skin?"

"I ate it," PJ said sadly.

"Awww…why PJ?"

"I was hungry."

"Oh…Is that what happened to the rest of your legs?"

"Uh-huh."

"Oh…PJ."

20.

"I can't believe you were scared of me," PJ said once they started walking aimlessly into the void. "You used to be fearless."

Fizzy laughed. It came out of her like a firecracker and reverberated off the shaky borders of this realm so hard it caused an avalanche. To her right, a second sun disintegrated like paper in a stream, burning bright as it went but dimming the scenery when it disappeared. She held her mouth with one hand, afraid to make another sound, but PJ stuck out its hoof, protectively, then assured, "That wasn't your fault. It happens from time to time."

She let her hand drop but she wouldn't take her eyes off where the second sun once hung.

"See. This is what I'm talking about." PJ said. "You used to be unflappable. What happened?"

She shrugged, then gave him a wry smile. "I ask myself that every day, PJ."

They walked all night, or what she considered night to be in this world. A second sun joined the lonely survivor and they swirled behind an invisible horizon as if they preferred to dance alone in their after hours. A dull red sky took their place.

They found a ghostly tent city inside a concrete barrier reef. And the spiritly transients welcomed them with their apathy before going on with their tasks. A few of them ate alone, a few of them communed and gossiped like there was still a tomorrow. Some did drugs inside their tents, some fucked, some slept. One spirit, who couldn't have been much older than herself, was reading a slightly worn children's book to her small child.

They took the unclaimed space towards the back, sitting with their knees to their chests, like the kids who watched other kids run around during recess.

"Do you remember how we first met?" PJ asked, out of nowhere. Its earnestness made her smile. They must have missed her.

Surprisingly, she did. "Jeanette summoned you to try and scare me into behaving better."

"She did," PJ confirmed, in a light voice. "And, as I recall, you tried throwing me out of the house!"

"I wasn't trying to share my room with no demons."

"You were the first kid to ever try to fight me for trying to scare them," PJ said fondly. "We had a lot of great times together."

Fizzy smiled. They did and a lot of them came back to her, more vivid and beautiful than if they were happening now.

"Where've you been, PJ?" Fizzy asked after the nostalgia faded into the cold present day.

"Your grandmother thought I was spending too much time with you. She thought…Oh what was the wording she used…"

"She thought people would think I was batshit if people knew my best friend was a giant horseman demon," Fizzy said, knowingly.

"Correct."

Fizzy sighed. Though she couldn't fault the woman for doing what she did, a small bitter part of her did anyway. Everything good and bad started and stopped with that woman it felt like.

"Where'd she take you?"

PJ's body slumped with new sorrow. "She gave me away."

"To who?"

"I don't know his name. All I know is…he owns a bar."

"What did he make you do?"

"He locked me away. Underground. And he would starve me for weeks on end. And the only time I was let out was to chase my food."

She almost burst out crying then and there but she had to ask first. She had to confirm her worst fears. "PJ… did…did this man…have red hair?"

"I don't know what red is." He said.

"Was his hair straight like mine?"

PJ studied her hair for a moment then shook it.

Eventually, he asked, "What happened to your grandmother?"

"Oh, she died," Fizzy said.

"Ah," PJ Clements said. For a moment she was afraid PJ would mourn for the old woman, or worse, ask her how she was feeling. But neither of those things happened. "Good. That explains why I am no longer bound to that horrible place."

Fizzy smiled. She knew that feeling well. She remembered the day she stopped living with Jeanette ended. She was twelve. And her grandmother was screaming at her about the way she was peeling potatoes. How she had to be the dumbest kid on the planet if she didn't know how to peel a potato properly by now. And she wouldn't let up about it. She just kept screaming nasty things at her. And normally those things would get to her. Normally, Fizzy would cry or shut down, sometimes she would say something back but that would always turn into a longer, louder fight that she would always lose. But that day, she didn't do any of those things. She simply finished the chore, went to her room, grab her backpack, and climbed out her window.

Jeanette knew right away what she was doing and she followed her down the block, yelling at her to come back in, to stop embarrassing her like this but Fizzy kept walking like she couldn't hear a thing. Finally, Jeanette tried tricking her. "Oh fine. Runaway! See how long you last living on the streets." She told her. But Fizzy didn't buy it. She told her to her face, "I'd rather live in a dumpster than live with you."

"You don't mean that." Looking back on that day, it was the first time she ever heard her grandmother sound unsure of herself. And one of the last things Fizzy ever said to her was, "Yes I do."

She didn't get far before the cops picked her up. She was so defeated that when they asked her where she lived, she didn't beg them to save her (she knew better by then). She simply gave them the address and watched her grandmother's wretched little house zoom closer and closer towards her. She already knew, before they got out of the car to talk to Jeanette, that she would kill herself that night. She'd wait until bedtime, sneak a butcher knife from the kitchen, lock the door and stab herself in the throat.

But something miraculous happened. Jeanette lied to the cops. She told them, "She doesn't live here. She lives with her aunt." And she gave them the address to one of her father's sisters. And they took her there and she lived there until she turned seventeen and moved out with Zeno and a couple of other friends.

"You're free again." Fizzy remarked once the reverie washed away from her. "You must be excited."

PJ didn't say anything for a while. By the time It spoke again, the dark red hour had faded into a gray-red morning. "Freedom means nothing when you're constantly hungry."

They sat like that, watching this realm change until eventually, PJ's stomach started to growl. It wasn't a low grumble. It was a lion's roar. Fizzy felt the hunger simply sitting beside it.

PJ stood up. "I got to go."

"Do you have to?" She pleaded. "Can't you just eat the guy?"

"If I eat him, who will feed me after he's gone?" PJ asked.

She didn't have an answer. But the idea of her childhood friend going back to her world, of Affidious tossing another poor person into PJ's gullet, shook her in ways she couldn't bear.

PJ turned away, to leave her, but she leaped where she sat. Her body flung sideways, hands outstretched until they caught onto PJ's cloven hand. This time, when the blood vessels sprung onto her hand, coiling her wrists, crawling up her limbs like sticky vines, she didn't struggle.

One second, she was Fizzy. The next she had hooves and they were hitting the steps hard, willing the body to move faster and faster, ignoring every single atom in her being that begged her—screamed at her—to reconsider. But she powered on.

Once her hooves touched the front door, she kept running. Even as the bitter winds sliced every inch of her flesh. Every movement was pure agony. But she kept going, rounding the back of the bar. Her speed slowed as her limbs writhed and all the voices in her head told her to go back inside. *Spare yourself,* they all screamed. The pain blinded her from rational thought. But her body moved towards the alleyway, towards the dumpster.

Blood poured onto the flurry covered ground, trailing behind her like an oil spill as she approached the dumpster. It took her an eternity to get to it but she did. Delirium set in as she crouched in front of the dumpster. She tried to raise her hand, to lift the lid off and climb in. But the pain, the loss of blood, was too great. The edges of her sight were crowded by grayness until—finally—she blacked out.

21.

Friday Evening

Fizzy was startled awake by the sound of someone tapping on the glass. She jerked forward, stunned to find herself in her car, the world swathed in the light blues that presided dusk, safe and sound.

Fragments of the dreams flitted throughout her mind. It felt so real. All of it. She turned her head expecting to see the bar but was surprised to find she was still at her apartment. She checked the time on her phone and let out a heavy sigh when she saw it was well past five pm. She had slept through her first day supposedly washing dishes for the nice bartender. A second, more urgent tap pulled her out of her self-pity and she looked out her window to find Zeno, red-faced and weeping.

She opened her door and before she could ask her what was wrong, Zeno flung her arms around her neck and pulled her into a tight hug.

"What's wrong, Jelly Buns?" Fizzy asked with alarm.

But Zeno was too distraught to explain and Fizzy rubbed her back until she managed to stop crying long enough to go into the apartment.

Once they were inside, Zeno explained, "Okay, so, no big deal. No big deal. But...I think your grandma sent the ghost of a Bosnian war criminal to haunt the shit out of us into going to her funeral."

Pause. "Wait, what?"

Zeno explained what happened on the bus and Fizzy listened, her chest tightening with guilt when she got to the part about the funeral.

"Do you think I should go?" She asked, her voice small and insecure like a child's.

Zeno stalled, torn between not wanting to say the wrong thing and wanting to be truthful. She considered her answer for a moment then said, "I think you should do what you think is right."

"What do you think is right, though?"

Zeno bit her lower lip. "I don't know. I mean, I know what kind of person Jeanette was and I don't blame you at all for wanting to boycott her funeral."

"But…?"

Zeno shrugged. "It's not up to me, Fizz. It's up to you whether or not you go." She reached over and gave Fizzy's first four fingers a loving squeeze, telling her, "Whatever you decide to do, I'll support you."

Fizzy looked down at their hands with darkness etched into her face. "I've been having bad dreams too lately." She looked into Zeno's dark brown eyes and asked, in all seriousness, "Do you think this karma for talking all that shit about Jeanette?"

Zeno thought this over then with a one-shoulder shrug said, "You know me Fizz. I'm not a superstitious person. But…"

"This is the wicked witch of the west side we're talking about." She said with a sardonic laugh. Then she sighed and said, "I don't know… Maybe I should go."

Zeno gave her a sad smile then hung her head as they sat together in silence.

Their silence was interrupted by the sound of Fizzy's phone going off.

They both looked to see Darlene's contact photo flash across the screen.

"You should call her back," Zeno said softly.

Fizzy nodded, then with a beleaguered sigh, answered the phone call.

22.

After an hour of screaming, crying, and tearfully apologizing to her mother for being so disrespectful, Fizzy agreed with a heavy heart to go to the funeral. As a show of apology, Fizzy baked her mother and her siblings a beautiful chocolate cake, scrawling the words "I'm sorry" in giant loopy light pink letters.

She stood back, allowing the frosting bag to hang by her side, like a well-loved tool, and admired her work. At that moment, she was proud. But it was only for a moment for it was followed by an incredible sadness, a sadness that came quietly but gut-punched what it touched.

Her hatred for Jeanette doubled in that moment, standing there, remembering all the horrible things that woman did to her family. The psychological torment she put her mother through to the point where nobody could stand up to her, not even in death.

How profoundly she despised that woman, whose arrogant withered face burned in her mind with the intensity of a supernova about to explode.

She looked over and saw her childhood self, standing in the kitchen, giving her a look of utter disappointment.

"What happened to you?" The invisible child asked, disgusted. "You used to be fearless."

Fizzy looked away, ashamed. What did happen to her? What happened to the little girl that always stood up to Jeanette? Even when all it got her was fists and curses, she never cowed to that woman in her life. So why was she kowtowing to her now? Who was she doing this for? For her mother or Jeanette?

"You should be doing this for you," her preteen-self sneered.

Fizzy nodded, slowly. *You're absolutely right kid.*

It was at that moment that she resolved she would go to her mother's house and tell the woman, with certainty, that she would not attend her grandmother's funeral. And she vowed, as she sealed the cake in a plastic container and gathered Zeno to leave, that no matter what she would stand by her decision.

23.

They left the apartment a little after the world turned dark blue and a crescent moon gleamed at them from behind light-pollution-made clouds.

For half of the drive, they said nothing instead of letting themselves get lost in Fizzy's playlist. Then the beginning of a song that Zeno adored caught her ear and she turned the volume back up, ready to annihilate the lyrics.

Just as the chorus was about to come and Zeno already had her mouth opened in anticipation Fizzy's hand stifled the rest of the song.

"Hey!" Zeno cried out. "That was the best part."

"Someone's following us," Fizzy said, her eyes narrowed onto the rearview mirror. Her back was flat as a plank and her chest was hunched over the steering wheel. Her hands white from gripping the steering wheel too hard.

Zeno's heart dropped. She turned over in her seat to see the car in question.

It was the most nondescript car she'd ever seen. Though she squinted hard at the front trying to identify the brand, she found no emblems, no familiar symbols, nothing. The license plates were nothing but framed paper and she couldn't see well enough in the nighttime life to see any numbers or letters. The most she could make out was the car was some kind of dark color—either a forest green or a dark red, maybe a maroon—but their headlights—two spotlights blazed into the car's interior forcing her to hold her hand up just to scrutinize. But there was no way. Her eyesight was too poor. The car was too vague.

The only thing she could discern was the sight of two shadows in the car, their bodies too blurry to be anything but menacing shadows.

"They've been on my ass since we left," Fizzy informed as Zeno leaned forward.

Zeno's heart was pumping at lightning speed. Every day, every day, she read those articles on what to do when someone tries to kidnap you. She read the survivor's stories. She studied the faces of the unlucky. She watched endless preparation videos. She bought herself self-defense classes for her last three birthdays. Yet all of that knowledge fled from her. Like cowardly rats, they scrambled into the farthest recesses of her mind and disappeared out of sight.

"Don't go to your mom's."

"I'm not," Fizzy promised. "I'm taking this left."

Zeno snapped the music off. They were dead quiet as Fizzy changed lanes, waiting until she was already in the right lane to use her blinker. Zeno watched from her side mirror, with the intense stillness of a cat, waiting for the car to confirm—or hopefully deny—their fears.

The car switched to the right lane. Zeno felt sheets of sweat accumulate against her back. She knew a panic attack was sure to come and she forced herself to breathe— ten seconds in, four-second hold, ten-second release— while Fizzy sped down two city blocks and, as if spur of the moment, yanked the steering wheel to the right down a road called Lamb Street. The right turn sent Zeno crashing into her door. Her face smacked into the cold window helplessly as gripped the plastic sides of her cake for dear life.

As the car straightened, Zeno looked into the mirror. What she saw made her heart slide into her thighs.

"Oh my god, Fizzy!"

"I know. I saw them!" Fizzy said, her back pushed into her seat, her leg stretched out and straight as an arrow. Her foot flat against the pedal. The engine roar as the car gained speed. Through clenched teeth, Fizzy shouted, "Fuck! What are we going to do?"

"Go to *Walmart*. There are way more cameras there."

"I can't."

"Why not?"

"Because I don't have enough gas to get to *Walmart*!"

Zeno sat up to glance at her gas gauge, it's little red light flashed at them rapidly as if the gas icon was screaming silently that it was starving to death. "Oh, for fuck's sake Fizzy!"

"I could have sworn I got gas yesterday!" Fizzy yelled back. "I didn't know I was going to be fucking kidnapped today!"

"Damnit Fizzy! It's like you don't even watch those anti-sex-trafficking videos I send you!"

Zeno looked over her shoulder. The headlights, golden orbs like two mini suns, trailed them. They were brazenly close now, less than a car length apart from the bumper. She whipped back around shoved her hand underneath her seat. Her hand slid back and forth frantically feeling for a weapon of any kind but coming up with nothing. "You have 20 *Dunkin Donuts* cups and a rubber snake back here but not any weapons?!"

"Stop yelling at me!"

Zeno pushed herself back into the passenger seat, her nerves aflame. She watched the car from her side mirror, her heart bouncing off of her ribcage. They passed five, six streets and the car kept on following, the headlights bared down on them like hate-filled suns.

Her mind raced. She glanced at the gas gauge and saw with horror as the little red arrow pointed closer and closer towards EMPTY. They had no weapons except keys and broken pens, not even a glass bottle or mace to hold them off. She looked over her shoulder trying to decipher how many were in the car but the night encapsulated them with anonymity. There could've been one assailant or four. Either way, they were fucked.

Then, she looked down at her lap.

Zeno groaned. "Fuck this." She said as she unstrapped her seatbelt buckle, then bizarrely, cracked the plastic lid off from the cake and tossed it over her shoulder. With one hand on the handle, her body upright and her knees sideways towards the door, she told Fizzy, "Slow the car."

"What?"

"I'm going to jump out and chuck this at their windshield."

"What?! No! I'm not letting you jump out of a moving vehicle! You'll shatter your ankles!"

"I did it before!"

"You were thirteen and lucky. You do that now and you'll explode on impact!"

"I'm twenty-seven, not eighty-seven, dickweed!" Zeno snapped.

"Doesn't matter! I'm not slowing down the car just to watch you get kidnapped! What if one of them jumps out and grabs you?"

"If you keep the car at ten miles an hour, I can throw chuck the cake at their windshield and hop back into the car."

"You're going to give them cake to deter them from kidnapping us?!"

"When the frosting hits their windshield, they won't be able to see shit. And if they try to use wipers on it, it's going to smear like a motherfucker on their windshield. They won't be able to see. It'll give us some time."

Fizzy balked, her mind too snagged on all the negatives to come up with anything better. And with the yellow gas gauge blinking at her furiously, reminding her that there was little time to argue, she relented. "Are you sure you can run ten miles an hour?"

"I can run twelve miles an hour," Zeno said, confidently. "And I'm wearing my good shoes."

Fizzy sighed, terrified. "Okay." She whispered as she tapped the brakes. The car eased from a gallop to a crawl. Zeno gripped the silver platter of the cake as she watched from her side mirror as the car behind them slowed as well. She hovered against the door, hand curled over the handle

Fizzy's hands shook against the steering wheel as the speedometer dropped from thirty to twenty-five to twenty to fifteen then—"NOW!"

Zeno hopped out of the car, the door left open, her nonslip shoes hitting the concrete like the hooves of a gazelle. She made four long-legged dashes over to the car, heaved the cake onto the windshield with both arms, and hurled herself around just as the cake exploded directly over the tempered glass. She whipped herself around, slipping for a second to her knees but heeled herself upward and back towards the car without missing a beat. She heard the car's brakes screeched to a halt as she leaped back to the rusted car, back into her seat, slamming the door as she did. Her body pressed into the seat as Fizzy slammed on the accelerator, sending the two of them up the street, taking the widest right turn she could manage down the next city road.

24.

The two of them sat there, breathing heavily, Fizzy's chest against the steering wheel, white-knuckled and eyes peeled as she zigzagged down residential roads, making sure to keep just thirty miles per hour so a cop wouldn't pull them over. Her eyes darted to the rearview mirror, then the side mirrors, then back to the rearview mirror as she drove until finally Zeno pointed and cried, "Thank fuck!" And in their windshield, a petrol station appeared.

She whipped the car into the parking lot without hesitation and pulled alongside the first open gas pump. When she cut the engine off, the two of them sat there huffing like asthmatics.

The second Fizzy felt her heartbeat at a normal rate did she lean over and give her best friend a giant hug.

"Thank fuck you're so smart and athletic and brave," She exclaimed.

"Thank fuck you made your mom an apology cake!" Zeno said with a nervous laugh. But her laughter faded into silence leaving both of them to stew in their fears. "We can't go home."

Fizzy nodded, her eyes focused on the bright lights of the gas station ahead of them. She popped open the door and announced, "I'll call Brynn. See if we can stay at their place tonight."

"Good idea," Zeno said quietly before the door slammed shut on her and she was left in the unbearable quiet of the car.

She checked her side mirrors, waiting for those dangerous headlights to make their second appearance as she listened to the soothing sounds of a car guzzling up fuel. After a minute or two of panic, she forced her eyes away from the mirrors and checked her phone. She discovered a missed call from a number she didn't know. She swiped past it, knowing it was probably a telemarketing number, then dialed her mother's number. Her mother picked up on the first ring.

"Hey, mama." Zeno began in Bosnian but her mother's loud voice blitzed out at her.

"Where are you?!" She sounded frightened as if she already knew.

"I'm at the gas station, why?!"

"Your house is on the news…"

25.

Even with the windows up, they could smell the
smoke a block away. Fizzy pulled onto their street and at
once they beheld what was left of their home. A charred
husk surrounded by its own carnage, encircled by a
squadron of firefighters who were already in the process of
packing up their tools. They passed by an ambulance where
Fizzy could see, with great surging relief, Grandpa Claus
smoking his pipe, tapping his foot, grumbling out nonsense
while his son Mario, sat in the back of the open truck
staring at the structural heap with watery eyes and shaking
his Buffalo Bills capped head. Fizzy gave them a stupid,
lazy little wave but neither of them returned it. Further to
the side, they saw their landlord in an animate conversation
with a person they assumed to be the fire marshal. She
couldn't hear a word he said but she could hear the

earnestness in his tone and she knew all at once he was covering all his bases. She could imagine the lies: "No, I had no idea what could have caused the fire. Everything was up to code, I made sure of that…"

Fizzy veered, wanting to go over and tell the fire marshal the truth but she was caught by Zeno's grip and when she turned her head to see the tears running down her face, the spiteful desire vanished. For a moment, they just stood there, staring at another. All at once, the rage was usurped by loss and then coupled with terror.

They were homeless.

26.

They walked through the line of neighbors who came to gawk at the tragedy from behind wooden blockades, too enwrapped with the wreckage to care about the women who wove between them.

Soot and ash landed on their faces as they approached what remained of 1215 Carter Street. Water ran over the smoking rubble and soaked the frozen ground. Siding mixed with broken support beams; shingles littered the front yard beside limps piles of the chimney; Fizzy saw a small patch of carpet stick out from underneath a broken window pane. The house laid before them a crumpled mess as if pushed down by a giant toddler. They knew, without being told, that there would be very little salvaging.

They stood there for however long, just crying and looking over the debris, until, eventually, the fire marshal came over and introduced herself to them.

Most of what she said was lost on Fizzy. She merely stood there, catching the tail end of everything she said to them. She was vaguely aware that Zeno was answering her questions for both of them. How they were gone most of the day and how they were on their way to her mother's when they got the call… Their conversation weaved in and out of her subconscious as she stood there, transfixed on the smell—the mixture of smoke and chemicals and watery ash—so strong it could feel it burrowing into the front of her skull.

27.

They sorted through the backseat of her car while they waited for Brynn to come and pick them up.

Zeno merely shoved things around while Fizzy hurled whatever she touched from the back of the car into the front of the car.

Zeno found a bunch of unimportant papers tucked into the kangaroo pouch behind the passenger seat along with six crushed up cans of energy drinks, a copy of a paperback book missing a cover, two pairs of work shoes that didn't fit her, three badges from workplaces Fizzy long quit, a green afghan, two lighters, four half-empty bottles of body spray, three pairs of ankle socks without pairs.

Fizzy tossed out a dozen old receipts, two snowbrushes, a broken flipflop, a pair of underwear that she hadn't seen in years, a beanie soiled by iced coffee spillage, and three grocery bags full of jeans that no longer fit that she planned on donating but never got around to.

The trunk offered nothing but a few scratched CDs, a tire changing kit that Fizzy had no idea existed up until that very moment, and a jug of windshield washing fluid which laid sideways in the farthest end of the trunk, mockingly.

"Find anything?" Zeno asked, listlessly.

"Na," Fizzy said. "Did you?"

Zeno shook her head, then started weeping.

Between the two of them, they had: less than 30 dollars, in person and the bank; their wallets; Zeno's backpack which carried her work clothes and her charger; and the clothes on their backs. Fizzy had less than Zeno. For the sweater, the leggings and the socks she currently wore were borrowed from Zeno's closet. All Fizzy had to her name was a winter coat with a stubborn hot chocolate stain on the front that dry cleaning couldn't get out, a pair of winter boots with a hole in the right heel, and a car full of trash.

They were weeping in her car when their downstairs neighbors approached the car.

Fizzy turned her car on and rolled down the window in silent misery. "Hey."

"My dad wanted to tell you something."

They looked at Grandpa Claus, who was sucking on his corncob pipe behind him. He took the corn cob pipe out of his lips long enough to say something Fizzy didn't understand at all. She glanced at her best friend, knowing she understood word salad but was stunned to see her friend's face pale and ashen. Like she had just seen her own ghost.

"Who told you to say that?" She demanded with an urgency that startled Fizzy.

"Uh," Grandpa Claus pondered for an uncomfortably long time, smacking his cracked lips against the wooden handle of his pipe as he thought before answering, finally, with some lucidity, "I don't know his name."

"Was it a bald guy?"

He nodded his head and their conversation ended there.

Fizzy waited until the father and son duo were out of earshot before she asked, "What did he say? You know I don't speak Schizophrenic."

"He wasn't speaking Schizophrenic." She whispered, terrified. "He was speaking Serbian."

This struck Fizzy as odd, for she knew Mr. Petito was Puerto Rican, not Balkan. But she stifled the fear rising in her throat long enough to ask, "What did he say?"

"He said," She gulped hard, her breathing unsteady and her face streaming with frightened tears as she struggled to explain, "He said, 'are you willing to die for your friend?'"

A cold fury circulated within Fizzy, contorting her face into something beastly and full of rage. She then pulled her phone out of her pocket and stabbed her screen ten times.

Two rings later, her mom picked up. "Hey, I just heard from Tonya. Are you—"

"Mom, do you know the name of the guy who owns *the Topspin*?"

"What? What does that have to--?"

"Mom, this is important. Do you know the name of the guy who owns *the Topspin*?"

"Uh, yeah, his name's Affidious Dixon. Why--?"

"I'll explain later." Then she added passionately, "I love you ma."

She hung up while her mom was still trying to figure out what the hell was going on, turned to her best friend, and said, "I know whose been fucking with us."

28.

Five minutes of internet searching and ten bucks later, they knew everything about the man: Where he worked; His criminal record; His social media posts about his struggles to lower his high blood pressure; Most importantly, his home address and his phone number.

They drove to the corner store and gave the man panhandling out front the last twenty dollars they had to borrow his phone for ten seconds.

Zeno made the call since he didn't know her.

After three rings, a man's voice picked up. "Hello."

"Anthony?"

"No, sorry, I think you have the wrong number."

"Oh, my mistake." She ended the call, thanked the man for his phone, and told Fizzy, "He's home."

"God bless old people who still own landlines," Fizzy said.

They went to Zeno's mom's first.

"Mom I need to borrow your guns!" Zeno cried as they stormed inside.

Her mom shouted out something in Bosnian.

"What did she say?" Fizzy asked.

"She said 'replace any bullets you use' and 'if the cops come by, I'm telling them you stole the guns'."

"You're the shit, Tonya!" Fizzy cried.

"I know dear!" Tonya cried in her heavily accented voice.

Fizzy pulled alongside a modest-looking two-story home. A newish looking car sat at the end of a long driveway. Fizzy took a few moments to stare at the smudges on the inside of the windshield, debating whether or not this was a good idea. She looked to Zeno and asked, "What say you, Zenny?"

Zeno held her gun, turned the safety off, and said, firmly, "Let's do this."

29.

It was nightfall and Affidious couldn't stop pacing. Every minute that went by felt like agony.

"Affidious, what's the matter?" Olivia asked from the kitchen table, her head bent over the paper she was grading.

"Nothing."

"You could've fooled me." She said drily. Her red pen slanted in her hand as she looked up at him and said, with a look on her face of inviting invocation, "You've been acting strange lately."

"No, I haven't," he lied quickly, his mind on the Wraith.

She gave him an unconvinced look which he ignored. She dropped the matter and returned to her work.

A knock on the front door made his pacing come to a screeching halt. The way he acted she would have assumed he heard a bomb detonate.

"Go upstairs."

"What? Why?"

"Just. Do. It." He had a look in his eyes she didn't like. He was afraid of whoever he thought was at the door.

She got up from the table and took the stairs. But she didn't go to her bedroom. Instead, she hid against a wall and he listened as he made his way to the front door.

"Remember me, asshole?"

30.

A commotion commenced. Whoever was at the door had forced their way in with a weapon. Affidious was saying, in a voice that didn't sound like him at all, "Whoa, whoa, whoa. Ladies, let's talk about this."

Olivia's spine rusted with horror as she asked herself, *what did he do now*?

"Okay. Talk. Tell us why you burned our house down. Tell us why you've been following us and why you've been trying to ruin our lives!" Zeno's crackly voice shouted.

"I have no idea what you're talking about…"

"Fuck you! You know exactly what we're talking about!" Fizzy screamed, unhinged with rage. "Why are you doing this to us?!"

"I don't know what the fuck you're talking about!" He boomed. "And who the fuck are you to come in here making all these baseless accusations?!"

Oliva winced. She knew he was lying. 'Baseless accusations' was his favorite term to use whenever caught in a lie. She knew he never admitted to his crimes either and knew, if she didn't go down there, she would end up hearing their guns going off and the sound of his body hitting the floor.

Olivia took slow deliberate steps down into the living room where she found her son being bound by the wrist and ankles by two young white women—one of whom she knew immediately.

Fizzy looked up in time from duct taping his wrists to catch the sight of the elderly Black woman with the horror-stricken face enter the living room. She froze upon seeing her.

"Oh, shit…" She murmured.

Zeno, who was still pointing the gun at Affidious' head, looked over her shoulder, and when she saw the elderly woman her heart sank to her feet.

"Oh fuck…" Zeno moaned. Then, with awkward cheerfulness, she said, "Hi, Doctor Dixon."

"Hello, Džejla," she returned, her voice was soft with barely concealed shock. For a while, the three of them merely stared at the other, too stunned to say anything. Then Olivia broke the silence with a small chuckle, adding, "How funny. I just got done grading your essay."

"Oh…" Zeno said, brightly. "What did I get?"

"Zeno, this is not the time," whisper-scolded Fizzy.

"Mom go back upstairs," Affidious ordered.

Olivia ignored him, keeping her focus on the two young women.

"Don't do this," she pleaded as she slowly made her way into the center of the living room. "I swear whatever he did…"

"I didn't do anything!" Affidious cried, offended.

"Oh, you lie every time you open your mouth!" She snapped her tiny black eyes narrowed on him with disgust. He quieted instantly and she turned her attention back to Fizzy and Zeno, shifting her gaze between them equally as she pled, "You don't have to do this. Whatever he did, I promise killing him won't make things better."

"Doctor, you don't understand…" Fizzy croaked, her blue-orange eyes running. She pointed at him with her gun-less hand and said, "This is going to sound crazy but-

but he's trying to kill us! All because I won't go to my grandma's funeral. And I need to know why!"

"So, ask him." She said softly.

Fizzy turned her head to Affidious and tearfully asked, "Why?"

Affidious looked at him mom, then at Fizzy, at Zeno, looked back to him mom, dropped his head into the cool floorboards and with a heavy sigh, said, "Look out the window."

With her gun kept on him, Fizzy inched to the window and drew back a sheer curtain. In the darkness, she spotted the car that was following them mere hours ago, idling, ominously.

"You know that guy that's been following you? The one that's been in all your dreams? The one they call 'the Wraith'?" Fizzy and Zeno nodded, dumb-tongued with fear. "He's a friend of your grandmother. And…if you don't go to her funeral," He took one last apologetic look at his mother and explained, "He's going to kill my mom. Possibly—probably—do worse things to her."

The air in the living room thinned as the gravity of what he said set in on the three women.

"But, but why?" Olivia breathed.

"Because…" He began, sounding like a man on his way to making a confession he hoped he never had to give.

31.

They met during his first year of owning *the Topspin* when the bar was hemorrhaging money. It was bad. Most days, the only ones who frequented the bar where the homeless, who mostly just used his establishment to wash, fuck, and do drugs in his bathrooms. He had just chased out two men who were fucking in the women's bathroom out when the sound of Jeanette's laughter caught his attention.

She was this little old thing: short blonde hair, bright warm blue eyes, plump with a round face that invited people to talk to her. She looked like Mrs. Claus.

"Every time I come into this place, you're chasing away a vagrant." She remarked once he took his position behind the bar.

"You're telling me." He said with an annoyed grunt.

She smiled at him, then looked at his nametag. She made a thoughtful noise. He waited for her to ask him the same inane remarks that usually come with white people finding out his name: "That's a mouthful." "How do you pronounce it?" "That's an interesting name." "Is it African?" "What does it mean?" "Ha, that sounds like a fancy version of Fiddy Cent's name." (One time a white man asked him, with actual wonder, "Are you Fiddy Cent's Dad?") But she surprised him by saying, "Like the Shakespeare character?"

"Yeah, actually." He said with a genuine smile.

"Oh…You poor thing." She leaned in and gave him a conspiratorial grin. "I bet both your parents were giant nerds."

He let out a hearty laugh, liking her instantly. "You already know."

He went on to tell her his life story: The difficulties of being the wayward son of two pillars of academic achievement and Black excellence; the bullying the came with his name, his hair, his weight, his dark-skin; his mother's late-in-life schizophrenia diagnosis; the early, unexpected death of his father; his struggles with eating; the pride of watching his lifelong dream of being his own boss come true; the crushing despair that came with knowing his dream will likely being deferred soon.

To Jeanette's credit, she listened and pretended to care.

"I put everything I had into this bar…" He told her at some point long after the bar was supposed to close. It was just them the whole night anyway.

"It sounds like you could use a little help," she said sweetly. "I can help you if you want."

"How?"

"How else? With the money of course. How much do you need to keep this business going?"

He told her the amount and to his amazement, he watched her dig into her purse, pull out a checkbook, scribble out the amount and hand it to him.

He was so stunned when she tried to hand it to him all he could do was stare at her. "Why are you doing?" He asked, touched by this stranger's kindness.

She gave him a closed-lip smile. "You remind me a lot of a friend I used to have. A friend that I haven't seen in a long time…" Her voice trailed off sadly as her eyes got distant and dreamy.

He reached forward to take the check when she pulled back her hand. "Not so fast. I need one thing from you."

Affidious sighed, disappointed but unsurprised. *There was always a contingency to white people's generosity*, he thought.

"It's nothing big." She said, reading his thoughts. "I just want to hear you say, 'I owe you'."

Pause. "What?"

"Three little words. That's all I want to hear. And the check is yours."

Affidious looked at the check which dangled in the air before him like a ribbon waiting to be snatched. But his mind was stiff with paranoia. Was his imagination getting the better of him or did her face change in that second, from the sweet little old lady into something sinister, something almost—demonic? He blinked and the sweet, little old lady visage returned.

"You don't have to pay me back. You'll never have to worry about interest rates. I just want to hear you say, 'I owe you'."

He looked her in the eyes. "That's it?"

Her tiny blue eyes shined like jewels. "That's it."

He thought it over but money won. As it usually does. "Okay. I owe you."

She smiled at him then handed him the check. He took it gratefully, thanking her profusely, as she gathered her things and headed towards the door.

"Hey, just call me," she said with a shark-like grin, "You're fucked-up fairy godmother."

From there began the start of a very lucrative, and very fucked-up, relationship.

32.

They listened to his story in enraptured silence.

Fizzy was the first to speak. "You could've just came to me and explained the situation."

"What was I supposed to say?" Affidious snapped. "'Hey, I know we've never met before but your dead grandmother said if I didn't make sure you went to her funeral, she'd have the ghost of a war criminal rape and murder my mom? I know that sounds crazy and I know if you did a quick background check of my family, you'd see severe mental illness runs in my family, but trust me? None of that's related?'"

He saw his mother wilt in the corner of his eye and it broke his heart but now was not the time to lie.

"Yeah, but..." Fizzy began, in a small, almost amused, voice. "This is Jeanette, we're talking about." He looked at her and saw the rage in her eyes from before was gone replaced by empathy. She looked back at him and her lips stretched into something of a half-smile. "I would've understood."

"In retrospect, yes, that would've been a lot easier," He admitted. A stretch of silence passed between them before Affidious asked, somewhat timidly, "So? Will you go?"

Fizzy looked at Zeno, who just gave her a look that said she'd support her no matter what decision she made. She then turned to Affidious and asked, "If I go, all the bullshit stops?"

"Yes."

She went quiet for a few seconds, then said, "I'll go."

"You promise?" Olivia asked.

Fizzy looked the woman in the eye when she said, "I promise."

Affidious' large body eased instantly at her words. "Thank you." He whispered. Then, in a louder empathetic voice, he said, "Thank you..."

PART THREE: RESOLUTIONS

1.

Saturday

Fizzy came to in her bedroom. A stray ray of sunlight broke through a nearby window and caressed the side of her face. For a split second, everything felt so serene and surreal, as if she had just awakened, safe and sound, after a horrible dream.

As if on cue, her phone went off beside her and she saw a text from Tranquila, which read, "Mom wants to know if you're going to the funeral."

Fizzy typed back a single word: "Yes."

They spent two full hours in preparation for the day: Zeno showered, shat, and brushed her teeth while Fizzy carved out a prettier face for herself, beating and baking and contouring away the angry cystic acne that trailed her cheeks and chin like an army of fire ants until her skin was airbrushed. Zeno did her makeup while Fizzy shoved herself into spandex until her stomach fat and their leg fat and their ass fat was slimmed and toned. Fizzy squeezed her breasts with wire and polyester until that fat was sculpted and lifted into something more acceptable while Zeno flat ironed her thick wavy brownie batter hair. They ironed the clothes they choose to represent their spurious grief: For Fizzy that was a black blouse covered in pink roses that covered her boobs nicely, a plain black skirt that fell to past her knees, and black stockings. For Zeno, it was her nicest long-sleeved black dress. They made their inspections, both on themselves and each other, lavishing each other with puffery.

Then, after all of that was done, did they finally smoke a blunt "in Jeanette's memory".

"Here's to you, Jeanette." Fizzy declared as she twirled the little brown stick over a mountainous flame. She took a long drag, until her lungs were filled with smoke, and exhaled into the floor.

"I like how you pointed your head at the floor," Zeno laughed as she took the blunt.

"Oh there's a Hell and she's there."

Zeno laughed pensively. "Yeah…I can already see her trying to make fun of Satan until they cried." Laughing harder at the idea, she added, "I can see her being the first person ever to get brought back to life because the devil didn't want her."

"Don't jinx us like that!" Fizzy cried, half-serious. "You better knock on wood because if she comes back, I'm gonna be so mad at you."

Zeno quickly knocked three times on the nightstand next to Fizzy's bed. "How much you wanna bet she's still going to torture us from beyond the grave?"

"Oh my god…" In her best Grandma Sobriquet voice, she mimicked, "'You guys called that a funeral?! I've seen better funerals for goldfish, you dickfucks!'"

"'Act like an asshole get treated like an asshole!'" Zeno quoted, laughing at her bad impersonation.

Eventually, they smoked the blunt down until it burned their fingers and they knew their allotted time was up. Then they sprayed themselves with sweet body spray until they were saturated and sticky with vanilla-and-pineapple sunshine (as if the girlie spray could mask the potent smells of whatever dankness their dealer offered that week), dabbed their eyes with redness relief, and exited

from the duplex to begin their afternoon of obligated
mourning.

2.

As a final fuck you to her family Jeanette Sobriquet
made it specifically known—both in will and in life—that
unless all her demands, however petty and ridiculous, were
met she would "spend an eternity finding a way to haunt
the absolute shit out of each and every one of you." She
wanted it all: the expensive coffin surrounded by a sea of
white lilies, an oil portrait of her likeness (from forty years
ago) on stand-by, her favorite song played on repeat and, of
course, a bodyguard with a list at the front door of people
banned from the funeral.

They made it to the funeral home five minutes later
than they were supposed to. The moment Fizzy cut the
engine off, she felt a piercing pain in her stomach. She
groaned pitifully

"Ah, shitnuggets." She whined, clutching her stomach, and leaning her head into the steering wheel.

"What's wrong?"

"I just got the Crimson Fuck You."

"Damn. Right now?"

"Uh-huh." She lifted her head and glared at the funeral home. "I don't know how but I know this is her fault."

Zeno frowned then turned in her seat and leaned herself over the middle divider until half of her was dangling in Fizzy's backseat. She used her hand to shove away trash and belongings, which mingled freely in Fizzy's car. Zeno dug far enough and climbed back into the front seat with an unopened menstrual pad.

"You're the queen of the century, Zenny," Fizzy said gratefully as Zeno handed her the product. She rubbed her aching stomach for a little way before she let out a low, contemptuous growl and announced, "Ugh...Let's get this shit over with."

They got out of the car and approached the entrance of *Sugi Pula's Funeral Home* only to be stopped by a bear of a man in a tuxedo with a clipboard in his furry hands.

"Names?"

"Da fuck?" Fizzy blurted out.

"I need names."

"What are you, a bouncer?"

"I need names."

"This is the deceased's granddaughter," Zeno said, pointing to Fizzy who also pointed to herself.

"You guys got IDs?"

"For a funeral?!" Zeno blurted out in a shocked laugh.

"We've had very strict orders from the deceased." The man replied flatly.

"Yeah but…" Fizzy began but cut herself short. Much like the bouncer, she also had very strict orders, from her mother, to not make a scene today. Besides, the man was only trying to do his job which she understood. She reached into her bra and pulled out her ID, muttering, "For fuck's sake."

Zeno did the same and the man took two seconds to scan over their names, then the list, then their names again. When he handed back Zeno's ID, he smiled at her name then joked, "Wow. That's a mouthful." Which made Fizzy and Zeno roll their eyes. He said nothing when he handed back Fizzy's ID. Then he took one step to the right, pulled the door open for them, and said, "Sorry for your loss." Zeno made sure to grab Fizzy's hand to suppress the urge, she knew she felt, to flip him off (This did not stop her friend from giving the man a lingering stink eye).

Once they were through the gilt doors and onto the purpled carpet, did Zeno say underneath her breath, "Not gonna lie, that was pretty fucking cool of your grandma to get a bouncer for her own funeral."

"Yeah…" Fizzy mumbled grudgingly. She hated saying anything positive about her grandmother, however small. "I just wanna know who she wanted to keep out so bad."

"Maybe she's trying to cull the number of people from spitting on her casket." Zeno peered over her best friend's sunglasses-covered face. "You're going to have to take those off at some point."

"No, I don't," Fizzy said, her head turned over her shoulder. "It's my grandma's funeral." In an off-key voice, she sang, "It's my grandma's funeral and I'll wear sunglasses if I want to."

"That's very true," Zeno said. She then gave her hand a good squeeze and added, "I love you."

"I love you too. Thank you for coming to this."

"Of course. Why wouldn't I?"

"I just appreciate you being there for me during all this." She said sliding her hand into Zeno's.

They proceeded down the same hallway and into the showroom the boxed-up corpse of Jeanette Sobriquet laid. The room was enshrouded in tiger lilies, pink lilies, white lilies, and wreaths that bore 'sorry for your loss' sashes. At the entrance stood a three-legged easel which carried an oil painting of a forty-something white woman with a platinum white bob, steel blue eyes and a don't-fuck-with-me scowl.

"Wow," Zeno remarked as she stared at the painting. "I had no idea your grandma used to be young. I just assumed she was born a mean old biddy." She turned to her best friend and asked, "How old was she anyway?"

"Old enough," said another woman's voice. Out from behind the painting came Darlene, a short, pink-faced auburn-haired white woman, followed by her other two children.

Fizzy propelled herself to her mother, whom she felt she hadn't seen in years, and the two of them hugged each other hard.

"I'm sorry, ma." She croaked.

"I'm just so glad you came," Darlene whispered gratefully into her hairline.

Fizzy murmured as she gave the woman a tight, shoulder hug. "How you doing?"

"I'm doing…" Darlene replied, her voice trailing off into something vague that made Fizzy's heart stir with worry.

"I can't tell if that's bad or not," Fizzy said, concerned.

Darlene's cheeks perked until they nearly touched her ecru eyes. "It's just been a hell of a week." Pointing her thumb to the painting she said, "You have no idea how much of a pain in the ass it was to get this stupid painting."

"I'm so sorry," Fizzy said, wishing she could offer something to take away her burdens and feeling helpless knowing she could do nothing.

Darlene shrugged. She looked as if she was going to say something else but changed her mind when Zeno stepped forward to get her a hug.

"Hi Darlene," Zeno greeted timidly. "I'm so sorry for your loss."

They embraced. Fizzy couldn't help but notice how pink her mother's eyes looked after they let go of each other.

"Thank you, chickee," Darlene whispered. "It's just been so much…" To her children, she said, in a voice light with mirth, "When I die, don't even bother with a funeral.

Donate my body to a teaching hospital and use my life insurance policy to pay off my debts."

"Okay," Tranquila replied. "But if I die before you, you better avenge my death."

"Don't talk like that, sweetie," Darlene said, annoyed.

"I mean it! The only I'm going out is if someone takes me out and you're going to have to be the one to seek vengeance on my behalf because we all know *Lonnie* won't." Tranquila said, cutting her brother a mock-heated glare.

"Don't worry TQ. I got you," Fizzy promised.

"See? Fizzy would avenge me!" Tranquila said to Lonnie in a bratty voice.

"I didn't see you avenging me when I almost went to jail for treason!"

This devolved quickly into squabbles which Darlene managed to silence with a single rattlesnake glare. Then she glanced at the clock and told the four of them to go to the bathroom now before the funeral started.

Fizzy and Zeno took her advice and went to the bathroom together. Along the way, Zeno said with a mushy voice, "I hope I die before you. I couldn't bear to lose you."

"Aww. That's so sweet. I always hoped we'd die together." Fizzy said.

"Really?" Zeno asked, endeared.

"Yeah. I always hoped it'd be in a car accident, but we don't see it coming because we're both too busy belting out to one of our favorite songs."

"Aww!" Zeno said, endeared. "I hope we grow old and stir up shit at the nursing home together."

3.

When they got back, Fizzy and Zeno took their positions besides Tranquila and Lonnie who stood on the small dais that showcased Jeanette Sobriquet's casket. Darlene was fiddling with her phone and just as they took their spots in the grieving line, music came over invisible loudspeakers.

A bee sting guitar boomed and soon the room was filled with the Elton John song, "the Bitch is Back"

Fizzy doubled over with laughter. "Great song choice, ma!"

"Actually," Darlene said as she stifled a laugh, "It was your grandmother's choice."

"No!"

She nodded. "It was her favorite song."

Fizzy shared surprised glances with Zeno, Lonnie, and Tranquila.

"Huh," Tranquila said. "Well, gotta give the woman credit where credit is due. She was self-aware."

4.

The doors opened to the public by nine am. By nine-fifteen am, two of the funeral home's staff were outside, checking IDs, reading through the list, holding the doors open for the dozens of people who huddled against another, in their winter clothes, bracing themselves against a cruel gust of wind that seemed to come for those who waited.

For the funeral people, it was a sight to behold: Lines of people, mostly older people with decaying faces, thick nicotine-stained teeth, and layers of coats on, came through, embraced Darlene, shook the four younger people's hands, made polite small talk and side-stepped over to spit on.

So many people came to spit on the casket, that when Tonya came to pay her respects, she asked her daughter, in Bosnian, "Is this a white-white person custom?"

"No, ma. She just sucked that hard." Zeno explained.

It made things a lot easier for the five of them. None of them got saddled with the tired phrases that bombard the survivors at funerals: Nobody said they were sorry for their loss (if they did, it was brazenly sarcastic, and promptly followed by fits of laughter); nobody asked 'how did she die' because, quietly frankly, nobody cared. They were just happy it happened at all; Nobody bothered with the 'she was such a lovely woman' 'she was one of my best friends' 'her laughter light up a room' lies. When Darlene had openly stated, how glad she was for her to be gone, not one person would have dared use the line 'well, she was still your mom' on her.

There were only two questions that couldn't be avoided, for, in these strangers' defenses, what else was there to ask. The sickly, uncaring, and banal, "How are you doing?" But even then, Darlene would look them dead in the person's eye, and say with a sad smile, "I'm doing." Then there was the more popular question, mostly asked by strangers visibly seething with rage, 'where's the burial taking place?' for they eager to fulfill their dreams of pissing, shitting, and or dancing on Jeanette Sobriquet's grave. But Darlene had to disappoint the masses by telling them that once again that horrible woman ruined their dreams by opting for cremation. How quickly these strangers fled the funeral home.

An hour into watching people pass by them just to spit on the closed casket, Zeno whispered to Fizzy, "Wow. I knew your grandma was mean but I had no idea so many people felt so strongly about her."

"Yeah…" Fizzy said with a pensive chuckle. "She had that effect on people."

5.

    The rest of the wake was uneventful. After the first forty-five minutes, the attendees dwindled dramatically. By ten-fifteen am, the funeral home was bare bones and by ten-thirty, Elton John's "The Bitch Is Back" was cut. Fizzy, Zeno, Tranquila, and Lonnie stepped away from their positions next to Jeanette Sobriquet's casket and took their places in the empty chairs where no one, except two funeral home staff members who stood solemnly against the back wall, and one purple-nosed man who sat in the very last chair, waited to hear the eulogy to the most hated woman in the city.

    Darlene stood before Jeanette's casket and addressed the room: "Thank you, everybody, for coming…"

"No, thank YOU!" The stranger cried, eliciting laughs.

"I just wanna say thank you for being respectful towards me and my family during this time. I know just about everyone here had ill will towards my mother but the fact that you were able to separate your feelings about her and be kind to us means the world to me. I know a lot of you have asked about her burial location. Unfortunately, she requested to be cremated so there will be no burial after this."

This caused the purple-nosed stranger to jeer.

"I know, I know, a lot of you had your hearts set on dancing and or shitting on her grave." She said with an empathic disappointment that told them all, *I was just as disappointed as the rest of you.*

"Anyway, I just want to say thank you again to everyone for being so kind and understanding to me and my family. I can't tell you how…happy I am to be standing up here." A tear sprung out from her right eye. She said in a voice crackling with joy, "Sometimes bad things do happen to bad people. And for once in our lives, we got to be there when it happened."

This caused the room to whoop and holler.

"I just want to end this eulogy with a quote I saw the other day," Darlene spoke once the cheers lulled. She pulled out a piece of paper from her pocket, unfolded it, and read, "To the living, we owe respect. To the dead, we owe the truth.' And the truth is, if anybody deserved to get struck down by lightning, it was Jeanette Sobriquet!"

Her speech, and the cheers that followed, could be heard by everyone in the funeral home, even the two doormen who stood outside smoking cigarettes. They eyed each other in alarm at the sonorous sounds of people happily cheering for a human being's death.

"Wow…" said one man to his coworker, disgusted to the point of near-speechlessness. "Disrespectful."

"They are the family," his coworker reasoned with a shrug.

The first man shook his head. "Doesn't give them the right to talk ill of the dead. This hands down the white-trashiest funeral I've ever worked for."

The other shrugged. "Eh, I've been to trashier."

6.

Affidious pulled his car into a sparse parking lot, watching his rearview mirror the entire way, waiting for the Wraith's car to appear. It never did.

Seeing the near emptiness of the funeral home delighted him most wickedly. He had to jam a fingernail in the space between his tooth and his gums just to get himself to stop smiling. Then, after a few practice rounds of saying 'I'm sorry for your loss' with a straight face, he unbuckled himself and made his walk for the front door.

A burly man with a clipboard tried to ask his name but Affidious slide him a few folded-up bills and went on walking. The only sounds he heard as he made his way to the showroom were the echoes of his footfalls and the silence, the absence of others, the sheer lack of grief, brought him malicious joy.

Within seconds, he was in the showroom with the many rows of empty white folding chairs and the brown-orange casket. Oh, how he dreamt about this very box. And how beautiful it looked to him then underneath the florescent lights, in a room bereft of mourners, on top of a hideous purple rug, and in a sea of dying lilies.

Affidious felt dust bunnies collect within his throat as he tried to open his mouth—to do what he hadn't thought that far—but every attempt he made to make a noise—to gloat or jeer or to just plain cry—he felt those little dust bunnies run to the back of his tongue and choke him.

It's okay, he thought as an involuntary urge to sob came over him, and sent his hand to lips to cover his silent tears. *It's okay now*.

But then a sickening fear weltered over him and stifled his sobs. *How do you know?*

He clutched his hand and pulled it into his constricted chest as he stared down at the coffin's lid. *How do you know for sure?*

He didn't. But he reached forward with both hands and grabbed the lid. He needed to peek because he needed to squelch the little voice in his head telling him to be afraid. He got the lid to raise and he had his palms dug into the border of the lid, his elbows propped and ready to lift it higher when a woman's voice rang out behind him and harked,

"She's not in there."

He jerked away from the coffin and let the top drop with a thunderous slam. He spun around and found himself in the presence of Fizzy.

"Also, I wouldn't touch that if I were you." She said casually as she walked down the middle aisle of chairs towards the front. "A lot…of people spat on that today."

Affidious stared at her while his heart settled back into its proper place. "I—um, I was just…"

"You wanted to make sure the wicked bitch of the east coast was good and dead." She replied. Affidious watched her reach down to retrieve a phone that was lying on one of the front row's chairs. She checked it quickly then dropped it into her pocket and continued, "A lot of people wanted to make sure. Unfortunately for y'all, she got cremated." She pointed to the coffin. "That was just for show."

Affidious glanced over at the coffin, which he now noticed little strands of spittle crawling down the dented sides and sitting on top of the coffin as if it rained indoors.

When he turned his head to look at this young woman, he couldn't help but smile. "Thank you again."

Fizzy gave him a modest smile. "Hey, no problem." She glanced at the coffin and said, darkly, "I get what it's like to be controlled by Jeanette."

A small awkward stretch of silence passed between them before Fizzy felt her phone vibrate against her thigh and she knew without looking at it, it was either Zeno or one of her siblings calling, thinking that would help her find her phone faster. "I have to go. But good luck to you."

Affidious stuck out his hand to her and said, as she slid hers into his, "Likewise." With that, she left him and once her footsteps faded into the void did, he turn around to face the coffin. He scrapped his throat clean of every ounce of spit he could muster and happily spat it all onto the unused pall-bearer rails. "I'll see you in Hell, bitch."

Affidious smiled ruefully as he left the funeral home. He wondered how pissed Jeanette would be if she ever found out that the horse-demon she "rehoused" all those years ago had made him a millionaire. The thought of her shadow, raging in the fires of a Hell he knew didn't exist, shaking her fists, cursing his entire life, comforted him.

He hoped there was a hell. He'd love to see the old witch again.

When Affidious got out of his car, carrying a heavy plastic bag in one hand, he turned his head in every direction, scanning the neighborhood for the Wraith. When the Wraith was nowhere to be found, he smiled. He walked with a spring in his step. Like the frigid air, the sunless sky, the winds, and the ice didn't bother him in the slightest. He sang a song under his breath.

When he unlocked the door, he sang louder until his untrained voice filled out every corner of *the Topspin*. Until the walls boomed with the sounds of his joy.

He was feeling so generous at that moment, that when he was at the store, he picked up a rack of lamb for the creature. *It deserves a nice treat*, he told himself as he descended into the basement.

He got to the second step before a heavy *THUD* shook him at the feet and made him pause. It took him exactly two seconds to realize what was happening—the demon's head poking out of the shadowy basement then the heavy, fearsome thuds that came as it came at him like off-white lightning.

Affidious didn't have time to move let alone scream, though he was able to get one word out before the demon's jaw unhinged and ripped his head off his neck like it was beef jerky. "SHIT!"

7.

April

Fizzy and Zeno stood on a crooked, lumpy sidewalk just before *the Topspin.* Yellow crime scene tape that bordered off the perimeter like a lazy haunted house. The crime scene was so fresh the detectives hadn't given up on finding a killer yet.

The two women huddled together, their backs towards the bar. Except for Fizzy's winter coat and Zeno's winter boots, neither of them wore black.

Fizzy unrolled the crinkly bag and held it out in front of her like a basketball before tipping it over and letting the gray contents spill onto the sidewalk like a bucket of sand. Then, she heaved the makeshift urn into the dirty slush-covered grass and cried, "Alright. The fun part!"

Immediately, the pair joined together in stomping the dusty fragments with great zeal. They stomped and kicked and jumped and rubbed it into the ground with their toes and twerked and jigged and then stomped some more. When they were done, their boots were completely gray but the pair was breathless with joy.

Affidious Dixon's body was discovered on March 29th two days before his forty-seventh birthday. Neither his killer nor his head was ever found.

CPSIA information can be obtained
at www.ICGtesting.com
Printed in the USA
LVHW021034110121
676185LV00002B/131